For Rudy,

CYBERWAR

Worlds change,
but words remain.

7/7/22

PENTIAN

CYBERWAR

By RJ Huneke

Published by **Pentian**, an imprint of Lantia LLC.

This book was made possible thanks to the contribution of the following sponsors:

Adrianna DiGiovanni
Anna Maguire
Mirza Basim Baig
Ninad Desai
Brian Stone
Heather Huneke
Helen MacDonald
Alyson Lamberti
Bruce & Michelle Jones
Cassandra DeMario
Cheryl Huneke
Dana Andreachi
Debbie Garlipp
Doreen Huneke
Helen MacDonald
Kurt Zisa
Sean Burton

A very special acknowledgement is granted to our top sponsor, who became a recurring villain in the series:

John Gersic

Lantia LLC
1321 Upland Dr
Houston, TX 77043
info@pentian.com

ISBN 978-16-35031-46-1

CYBERWAR

R.J. Huneke

This book is dedicated to my love, my soul, Cassie.

ACKNOWLEDGEMENTS

This book is the result of years of research, years of writing and editing, and most importantly a lifetime of good people helping me along the way. For all of my friends and family, you have helped me in more ways than I could ever put into words, and despite that I am going to try to verbalize some of my warmest regards anyway. I will ask that you all listen to Bob Dylan's "If not for you" to truly get the right feel for this.

Firstly to Liz Kaempf, I would not have been able to have such a congealed and sensible manuscript without your talented editor's efforts; thank you so much for the read, critique and edits. To my dear wife and my dear Mom and Dad (x2 now!) and my dear grandparents, and my dear sisters you have helped shape me into the person and writing implement I am today, and it means the world to me. To Laura Williams for being one of the first to read the finished manuscript and to love it, thank you for all of the years of encouragement. To my Aunt Karen, Uncle Tony, cousins Kim and Diana, my Aunt Nancy and all of my family across the wide universe that have been a positive force in my life, your support has been an invaluable source of strength. To my close friends who have over the years become family, I would not be here without you; specifically, thanks to Kurt Zisa for your advice and encouragement over the idea of Cyberwar, thanks to Gerry and Leslie Ditto for your friendship, philosophy, and art (and shared love of hockey), thanks to Cole Fleming, Anthony Kouris, Chris Weeks, Dan Peters, Dan DiDosti and all of your better halves for an endless source of inspiration and for keeping me alive over the years, and special thanks to Matt Doyle, my brother from another mother and his entire family, the MacDonald clan, who have adopted me as one of their own, and thanks to my Stony Brook (and now

Comic Con) brethren Sean, Maria, Liz, and all of you who I have had the privilege to meet and converse with at SBU. To all of my teachers and professors, past and present and there are many of you (you know who you are), you have fueled my writing fury and your tutelage made this all possible, especially Mrs. Geller who blew the doors off my hinges with the possibility of writing creatively at a very early age. To all of my myriad influences, especially J.R.R. Tolkien, Stephen King, George Orwell, Ray Bradbury, Isaac Asimov, Bob Dylan, Neil Gaiman, Philip K. Dick, Ralph Waldo Emerson, Omar Khayyam, Arthur C. Clarke, Katsuhiro Otomo, David Lloyd, Alan Moore, Frank Miller, Stan Lee, Steve Ditko, Jim Starlin, Joseph Campbell, George Lucas, Quentin Tarantino, Edgar Allan Poe and countless others, you are such a source of living, education, and infinite hours of joy, thank you.

I want to give special thanks to Enrique Parrilla and the entire team at Pentian for making this possible. And last, in the place of honor, I must thank my close friend John Gersic for spending hundreds of hours, at the least, reading, critiquing, talking over, and spurning ideas and great story every week – you never cease to ask me for more, your mind is genius, and I would not have been able to do this without you.

PROLOGUE

It all went to hell when the world's greatest cyber-warriors chose to wage war for themselves and not on behalf of the politicians that hired them. Hackers, they used to be called. Somehow the term for "one who hacks a computer"was deemed offensive during the Occupancy War and subsequently placed on the Banned Vocabulary List.

Many decades earlier, at the end of the twentieth century, cyber-warriors were defined simply:

<u>Cyber-warrior</u>

<u>Noun</u>

> *1. Cyber-warrior is a person who engages in cyber-warfare for personal reasons or out of political or religious belief.*
>
> *2. A spy that can infiltrate the highest levels of security*
>
> *3. Cyber-warriors wage war using information technology and may attack computers or information systems through hacking or defending them from their counterparts.*

1

THE DEVIL'S SHED

There was an overlong shadow just outside of the Devil's Shed. The facility's alias was local folklore; the graying storage container's door had what looked like two demonic horns of rust near the top. No one in town knew its real purpose.

William Waltz squatted just below the enormous demonization and waited patiently. His face was covered in grease to eliminate any glare that the rain might make on his skin; this was nothing unfamiliar to him, as his father had a career as a bike mechanic and in his short life had shown 'skinny William' the value of getting dirty when it served a purpose. Thirty years of grit had made him a world-class locksmith.

The code magnet had to pull enough of a reusable ocular scan from memory to fool the door's access scanner. The lock's subterfuge, a functioning power switch box, hung open from hinges. The box's red handle remained in the *off* position as a decoy.

Waltz held the B9 scatter pistol as though it was glued to his right hand, and he stood utterly still. In the sweeping rain, the only streetlamp was a good fifty yards away, and though the glint of its light could be seen in the drops that clung to the silenced black barrel, he was effectively invisible if he did not move.

Twenty minutes had already passed this way. The customized code magnet would infiltrate the scanner's memory sometime within twenty-five. *Come on already. I really have to take a leak*, he thought wryly. Sitting still was not one of his favorite tasks.

With an eerie scarlet glow the marble-sized magnet began to replicate the correct ocular image to fool the door. Waltz had already hacked the enemy's security network and looped their surveillance cameras so that no one would see him crouched beside their secret entrance.

The code magnet ceased giving off the red glare and gave a single yellowish flash at the door's ocular box. A general in the Cyber Arms division of I.C.E. appeared to stand before the automated programming, or at least a part of him did. The door, having seen an authorized member's eyeball and palm print, unlocked. There was a click and a hiss as the airlock was broken. *Thank you, General.* Waltz gave a salute to the device before it disappeared into the left hand pocket of his pants.

He pulled down the handle and light seeped out, inch by inch, revealing the black suit and the glint of his green eyes. A long cement staircase went down a couple of stories, at the least, before it was lost in the darkness of the bunker. His mission before him, the spy hurried inside.

2

STEPS

Something was off. There should have been guards posted at the bottom of the stairs, regardless of how secret the lab was supposed to be. As soon as Waltz walked into the dark, a single light above him shone down, like a spotlight, and illuminated the step in front of his feet.

Two steps down, after two more lights had lit, he halted. Staring at the cement surface revealed a deeper shadow between two of the stairs. The bottom of the second step did not entirely meet the top of the third one down. A crack spread out evenly. The building plans he had studied earlier corroborated the solid, cement-poured piece of architecture.

Then the space is a cosmetic wedge and nothing more?

He tried to ignore his instincts.

They didn't lay down a welcome mat for me he thought with a smile.

Waltz rummaged in his pants pocket and pulled out a pen with the caption "NEED COFFEE" written on its hilt alongside skull and crossbones. It had outlasted a seven-year warranty. He held his breath and tossed the trusty companion down to the third step.

The rectangular step sprang upward and from underneath its base dusty wires birthed segmented mechanical pieces that turned into an electrical set of robotic jaws. The shining silver teeth of the bot snapped shut on the pen, splintering it. The stepbot then leaned forward and bent side to side sniffing out any other potential trespassers.

"Jesus!" cried Waltz. He could not help himself.

"I had that pen for seven years, damn it!"

The exclamation went unnoticed. Luckily the false step did not have any functioning microphones to provide it with hearing. The machine resembled a centipede that took on bear trap qualities of snapping teeth. Its wires fell amongst many small metallic feet, and as it became satisfied that nothing was stepping near, the robot disassembled and folded its teeth away and below the cement step that resurfaced to take its place in the staircase. Pieces of plastic were littered on the stairs below.

God damn it! How could they possibly rely on an autonomous killing machine like this? thought Waltz.

It could go off on its own and murder everyone in the place.

He quickly took from an inner coat pocket a device that resembled a large silver pen. The cap twisted and a tip protruded from the bottom of the writing utensil, and though there was ink in it the writing implement had another purpose altogether. The pen's point neared the false step and detected the robot's electrical blood and shot a cloud of lightning that immersed the creature in an isolated EMP (electromagnetic pulse).

Waltz did not like to rely on the pulse. EMP's were in every cyber-warrior's arsenal, because their discharge could stop electrical machines, at least temporarily. But they often failed when they were needed the most, and people had recently begun to be able to revive zapped machines with a reboot tool that jumpstarted them. Very few had portable EMP's, like he did, because they were terribly expensive, illegal black market tools that were leaked by the same commercial giants that fed the Cyber war machine in the western hemisphere.

To Waltz's utter horror the stepbot did not die but instead leaped up at him to snap angrily. Its legs gyrated frantically as the two arms of fierce bear-trap teeth extended and tried to clamp onto his nose.

He jumped back in surprise and in one decisive stabbing motion plunged the pen, like a sword, into the gleaming crimson eye at the center of the dusty bundles of wiring. The creature froze in midair; the silver spear sizzled in the eye and power supply, and then the stepbot fell down the flight of stairs, dead. Sheer reflex and instinct had saved him.

3

THE BROTHERS

The flight home had been quiet in comparison to the noise made in the Devil's shed. Between the adrenaline flow from the successful mission and thoughts of the weird new robot that was EMP-proof, Waltz could not sleep. Despite helping himself to some of the private plane's vintage bottles of scotch and reclining back on the dark, empty cabin, it would not happen.

"Call Douglas X2327X" he said aloud. There was the chime of gongs as a ringtone.

"Will! What's happening, my man?" said Doug. An image appeared in the seatback in front of Waltz. A thirty year-old man who had ignored his shaving razor for a few days sat at a desk.

"I see you're not aware of the time back home, because it's two in the fucking morning."

"Were you sleeping Doug?"

"Nah, but I could've been" the two of them laughed.

"Me neither" said Waltz.

"No offense, but you look like you could use some sleep" said Doug.

"I'll sleep when I'm dead." Waltz raised his glass to the screen. "Cheers."

"Everything go alright over there?"

"It did. Some strange happenings, but it went well. I might have to get your brother involved when I get back."

"May the Force be with you"said Doug with a snort of laughter. "Better you than me."

"Thanks." Waltz sipped his cocktail and then watched the whiskey ball of ice rotate as he stirred.

"I got to tell you, there's been some messed up things going on behind closed doors where I'm working out of."

"Like what?" asked Waltz. He watched as Doug scratched beneath his chin nervously and then rubbed his eyes.

"Messed up things. I don't feel comfortable talking about it over the phone, even on a secure line" he said morbidly. "But hey, maybe I'll be up for a promotion after I complete this, and then I can go all over the world sipping drinks from the privacy of an empty jet."

"Maybe, you will" said Waltz.

* * *

The office was a labyrinth of cubicles and glass, and he found the labs with little difficulty, despite the jet lag. Memorizing building plans was an instinct engrained during cyber-warrior training.

"What the hell is it?" asked Waltz. He dropped the heavy case onto the steel bench and tilted it to dump out the contents.

"Got me" said Jordan. "You sure your EMP went off in the Devil's Shed, Will? Because I just don't see how that's possible."

"Yeah, I am." His tone was one of contained anger and feigned patience. His plane ride from the Wangluo (网络) government's facility in the heart of Beijing had lasted ten hours, and he had not slept a wink with the carryon duffel bag containing the robotics stowed behind his feet. Saving the world was not as glamorous as the popular James Bond films made it out to be.

Jordan buried his hand into the device's open metal casing and sifted through many wires of red, yellow, green, black and orange colors. He was only a Cyber Programmer, which meant that he, along with all of the Spies (the topmost rank for soldiers without real computer skills) was outranked absolutely by the cyber-warriors (the spies with skill sat one place removed from Cyber's Elite echelon itself).

And he was supposed to take what a superior said without question, as if it were written law. This was a point with which Jordan would never concur, or even acknowledge, since he and his brother, Doug, were the most talented programmers to ever grace the Cyber society. At the young age of twenty, everyone put up with Jordan, because he would either desire fieldwork as a cyber-warrior or just jump right up into the Cyber Elite echelon that ruled most of the Western Hemisphere from Canada to Peru. Such caste skipping was normally impossibility, but the very best forced their sheer talent forward. The Cyber powers that be felt that Jordan could do so when he felt ready, as his bloodline was valued almost as much as his work was.

Bits of foam insulation were pulled and tugged until they detached from the glued sidewalls of the casing and came loose. Jordan tossed them onto the wooden workbench without a second thought.

In Cyber, democracy was adopted and inherited from the former United States government's values. All people were created equal and judged equally, from the northernmost Canadian tundra to the southernmost tip of Peru under the Cyber State's Constitution. But there was one catch: all who excelled at computers from age one and on rose higher in the Cyber caste system, and though there was the guise of a democratic republic, the reality was very few ruled over everyone.

It was said that anyone could break into the Elite ranks by proving themselves hacking their way into the Cyber Elite's servers but only if they had programming prowess. Their exact numbers were unknown but few made it so far; one day M.J. might actually make it – Jordan nicknamed himself M.J. after a former basketball star that history tapes largely considered the best to ever play the game – or he might just forever be a pain in the ass to everyone that had the joy of working with his kind of undeniable genius.

"If I'm to believe you, William"

"I've never steered you wrong before." Jordan rose up from the steel workbench and looked at him with his head tilted thinking.

"You know, you're right" he said seriously. "Then believing you, William, I am going to assume that this stepbot, as you so aptly describe it, has some kind of defense mechanism that no one has ever seen before."

"Someone's seen it before, M.J." barked Waltz. He was only a decade older than the short programmer, but those years had offered more wisdom through experience than Jordan would ever be able to fathom, unless of course he left his bench and went out into the darker world beneath the sky as a cyber-warrior himself someday.

"Well I've never seen it before. And you're well aware of my track record studying every line of code and every schematic of robotics, past and present, that's ever been recorded" he said, and Waltz was.

"You say the EMP pen discharged fully, meaning you saw the discharge cloud of lightning, and not only did it not affect this little monster, the stepbot actually went immediately into attack mode, which means that it detected the pulse and had an instinctual protocol programmed in to make it react to and turn on the source of the offensive threat."

"How do you say so much without taking a breath?"

"It's a shame you had to go and destroy the CPU processor and the power supply all in one blow. I would've loved to have had this guy alive to play with" Jordan's demeaning tone implied that Waltz's technique of defending himself was barbaric and unnecessary.

He was just about to utter "if you had been there and had this thing nearly bit your face off" when Jordan who had bent over the bundle of wires and started rummaging around again cried "eureka!"

"I've never seen anything like it. A reverse pulse mechanism controlled by a damn strong and isolated magnetic pull. Do you know what this means?"

"That you've just gotten your rocks off in front of me?" asked Waltz.

"This stepbot was given an electromagnetic pulse-proof force field that was somehow created by a mix of magnetism and electricity to protect this little guy from your EMP blast invisibly. The field's probably not even physically there, as far as we can tell, but it's protected from all of our most lethal electronic weapons. If I can reverse engineer this tech... this will be revolutionary!"

Waltz pulled his sleeve cuffs further out of the end of his jacket sleeves and his thin clean shaven mouth twisted up at the corners in a tight lipped smile. *Making history should get the boss off my back for a little while*, he thought. *I could use a long weekend.*

* * *

After sleeping for an entire day thanks to a sleeping aid, Waltz was woken by a vibration coming from his smart-tab. He lifted a single headphone and placed it in his ear; from its front end a beam calibrated a holographic screen in front of his eyes. If anyone else had been in the room, the back of the virtual screen facing him would have appeared fuzzy and indiscernible.

Waltz watched as a crystal clear image of a dark-skinned, white-haired man sat in a comfortable looking armchair and scratched a short, white beard. It was Jon Enzo, his handler. He laid out the parameters of an emergency mission that needed to be carried out that night. He spoke quietly and methodically of the situation, the loss, and the solution. Hell had come to Waltz.

He had no idea if Enzo was one of the Cyber Elite, and none of the other cyber-warriors had ever heard or seen of one. But Waltz could not see the Elite revealing themselves to one such as him before he joined their little club. All he knew was that though the entire Cyber government worked for him, he worked for the Elite and the Elite sent their missions through Jon, paid him through Jon, and Jon had been the one who he had reported all of his successes and all of his failures.

"Discretion must be used" said Jon. Tears worked their way down Waltz's cheeks; he did not bother to wipe them off. Having finished, the old man adjusted his bow tie and sat back to lift a glass to him in some sort of library.

"I am sorry for your loss, William. But this has to be acted on immediately."

"Let me do it" said Waltz.

"Surely someone less close to the situation could"

"No, I'll do it."

"Then go now and sleep later. I was hoping you'd want to take care of this yourself. Use your pain to your advantage. And do it right. We can't afford another minute" said Enzo emphatically.

Waltz rubbed his eyelids with his forefingers. His face burned. The tears would not stop. His only friend in the world was gone forever. He was not sure if coffee was going to cut it.

He turned the coffeemaker on, rushed toward the bar, and tripped over an empty bottle. That decided him. He wanted to be sober for the mission. He wanted to remember it... the revenge.

4

THE NEW MISSION DEBACLE

The bookshelf was old. Some of the clothbound books were ancient. He picked up a childhood favorite, Tolkien's "The Hobbit", and saw the printing was from 1937, from the last century. Reaching his long arm to the back of the shelf where the book had rested, Waltz pulled and released the locking mechanism. The heavy wooden bookcase lost its rigidity and began to swing outward.

With a careful tug, Waltz silently swung the secret door open. He stooped below the brick top of the frame and climbed into an enormous office that took up much of one floor of the skyscraper. The entire side was clear glass lit up by the rising peaks of neon architecture. Few buildings went unlit in New York City at any hour of night. Darkness was kept distant.

Behind a fifteen foot wide oak desk sat a middle-aged woman that gaped at him as he entered the room. At first she fumbled for the red security alarm button underneath her chair. She pressed it repeatedly, but it did not respond. Her long gray hair was in a ponytail that swung from side to side as she tried to press the deactivated button frantically.

"This is quite an office you've got here" said Waltz coolly looking from side to side in feigned admiration of the lofty architecture. "I'm a little jealous. Not just of the view either, Helena, but of the bookcase. I'm a hobbit fan from way back." He smiled coldly to let her know that he was not messing around, no matter what he said.

"I'm glad you like it, um-uh, William, isn't it?

"It is" he said.

"Tell me, why would our friends in the Cyber Elite have the need of visiting me at this hour, William?" asked Helena.

"I'll answer that question and any other you might have. But first you have to give me something... why would a corporate CEO and essential ruler of a small group of North American communications conglomerates, and trillionaires, feel the need to bribe more services out of a government programmer? More importantly, who else besides Cyber Programmer Douglas did you put on your side project?"

The color drained from her face. Negotiation had long been a strong suit of a technically backward upper-middle class made up of gluttonous CEO's, so she knew he was not guessing when he had spoken. She had deceived far too many for far too long to not recognize the truth of knowledge, particularly when the public squandered a small percentage of income earnings on the myriad products, services, and distractions that society required of the faithful Cyber citizen and that she herself fed them. Her eyes flashed in the dimly lit open air as she thought of her next move; her side of the metaphorical chessboard looked beleaguered to him.

"Douglas is unable to speak, is he?" Helena asked quietly.

"You know that damn well" Waltz was unable to check the anger boiling out of his words.

"I'm sorry but if our mech-warrior division is to compete with the arms depot cells pooling together with I.C.E. in Tokyo, Cairo, and the EU in London to those fully backed by the Wangluo government in Asia, then I need more knowledge of what their top corporations are doing. I need to know what to move forward and backward on. The Elite do not wage war without a plan, and I haven't been partial to their plans for some time now. I cannot conduct business without similar contingencies."

"Bullshit" said Waltz slowly. "You already know all that I or anyone else in Cyber can tell you...legally" he said quietly, regaining his composure. His job required him to be calm and composed at all times.

"The twelve programmers assigned to your multinational corporation are more than any I.C.E. affiliation could ever show for their useless corporate powers. Or at least they would be useless if you were not feeding Wangluo information."

"I'm asking you again, have you turned anyone else? It could reduce your sentence. You may not realize this, with your warped egotistical perspective, but those cells are preparing to overload and meltdown fusion reactors in half a dozen places around the world while they simultaneously initiate outbreaks of an as of yet unknown super virus thanks to your ability to take our most talented programmers and somehow brainwash them to the point of fueling the guerilla terrorist attacks that are nearly underway. You know what they'll accomplish, don't you? You know what their endgame is?"

Her face went ashen gray and she swallowed.

"Please understand, William"

"You sanctimonious ass, you don't get it do you? Wangluo's race to take us down, here, at your birthplace, and place it under their governing body... they will kill everyone who opposes them."

"You don't know what I've learned" she said.

He looked away from her and around at the bright buildings and felt like he was on a low hanging cloud in the middle of the city. There was surrealism to the moment and an odd sense of *Déjà vu* that he could not fathom. They were so high up in the air of the physical world.

"I understand it perfectly. You have what most people on earth dream of, mountains of cash, and subordinates, and a view. But that's not enough. You'll never have real power because you can't do anything worth a damn where it really counts... online" he said. "You know all too well about the democratic illusion. Now who else did you bribe?"

"There was no one else."

With that denial, an angry scowl brought a deep red back to Helena's cheeks. She pushed on her desktop and pulled a scattergun from out of a hidden desk compartment that sprang from the antique wood. She aimed it at Waltz and squeezed the wide double trigger. He raised his hands, palms outward.

"Don't do anything so brave" Waltz said softly.

"I know why you're here, but you won't kill me. And they won't ever find me… not where I'm going."

"Mars hasn't been approved for civilian housing yet. Trillions of dollars in your account and you're already dead."

"Fuck you" she spat. The pistol shook in her hand.

The gun went off and blew up in her face. Pink skull and brain splattered the glass behind the desk and glowed obscenely over the vibrant colors of New York. He had epoxied shut the end of the B9's barrel when he was up to do reconnaissance earlier in the evening. When she pulled the trigger, the gun exploded in her face. There were no limits to the uses of five-minute epoxy.

His actions were not murder they were self-defense. He would have much rather had her live so he could watch her slow interrogation start with intimately placed bamboo reeds.

"You too" he said with a small smile. Doug would have appreciated his comeback one-iner. Waltz's eyes blurred with water, but he did not cry.

5

CORPORATE ERASURE

The bang from the gun blast was deafening. The body hit the floor hard, but Waltz did not hear it. He turned away from the crumpled dead and gave the finger to a white security camera that hung from the ceiling over the desk. The hologram device on his collar projected a cascading menagerie of Internet videos that made up a face shield and confused the camera. Those reviewing the tapes would note the callous hand and the giant square mask of videos that encircled his head.

Word about the assassination would get out, of course; it was just the proofs that had to be foiled. They would know the name William Waltz, cyber-warrior, and they would know what he did.

Corporate erasure, thought Waltz. Anger swelled in him.

In order to sleep soundly at night, he did the research of every assignment and every mark himself. He took the unpleasant assignments, followed the living dead firsthand, and applied a fierce scrutiny to their character until he was satisfied in the guilt and horrendous nature of the dangerous crimes they had, without a doubt, committed.

There had not been an innocent, or even a morally human target given to him yet. But this was different. Caches of lethal ammunition linked back to Helena. But worse than that, she had murdered his only friend. Waltz shook his head.

He had known the programmer, Douglas, since they were kids in middle school. He was probably the closest thing Waltz had to a real friend. And because of that he had dealt patiently with Jordan too, since they were brothers. They had been two of the most gifted brothers that the Elite had ever come across, and if they had kids Cyber would surely be watching the family closely to lay invisible claims.

Douglas's expertise had even saved Waltz's life, one time, when the office alarm had a system error and refused to accept his password. It would have set off the mining quadrants surrounding him, if not for the younger man's ability to near instantaneously hack the Cyber system and override security.

Waltz's best friend washed up on the south shore of Long Island and was recovered before anyone had known he was missing. Douglas's tongue had been torn out. From the evidence of bleeding and the expression, he had been alive when the bastards did it.

Wangluo's puppet mech-arms corporation wanted everyone to know to keep quiet; otherwise, Helena would silence them, bury them in the sand where they would stay until one of the areas frequent warm weather storms swept up the Atlantic and ripped them from the eroded remains of L.I. lowland, as it did every other week it seemed.

6

SHOTS OF RAIN

Rain fell to the glass wall in a splash. The ringing in Waltz's ears had not subsided, but his hearing had largely returned. He had to remember earplugs for close gun work.

How long had he been standing there, alone in his house, he was not sure. The last look was supposed to calm him, but instead the swelling Sound smashed the north shore cliffs and roused a fury he did not know existed. He saw visions of Douglas out there floating with seaweed entangling his dark curly hair and looked away. He had been cremated three days ago.

Waltz sneezed and doubled over. A pop and clink sounded. A spidery hole marked where a sniper shot had pierced his office window. After dropping to the floor, he crawled to the brick fireplace behind him. Luckily, the fire had not been lit since the night before. He wormed his way under the wooden mantel and crawled over the charred logs and ashes. At the back of the fireplace, he leaned up against a heavy stone tile.

After a decisive shoulder throw into the indented slate, a gap appeared between the back wall and the surrounding brick frame in the fireplace. Waltz saw two more bullet holes in the window before he turned and pushed through thick nets of cobwebs. His home was under attack. He started down a stone stairway and descended into darkness.

7

THE ROUND ROOM

Three and a Half Hours Earlier:

"I'm making this a vendetta" said Waltz. A general uproar followed in the dimly lit Round Room of the cyber-warriors. "It is personal for me" he admitted. Speaking in that room full of people made his throat as dry as chalk.

"But it's also an opportunity to make a statement to all of our adversaries across the Atlantic." said Ro "To whomever the hell we want. We're on to their alliances. Plainly put, we're coming for them. They're not the only ones that have the ability to infiltrate the world's biggest corporations and control the government's highest ranking individuals there."

A second stammering mix of voices vied for the floor. The cyber-warriors meeting was, at its smoothest, an attempt at organized chaos. This was, for the Elite's handpicked leaders of the Digital Branch, a normal process of business. After all, the cyber-warriors primarily acted from the shadows, alone. Meetings were abhorred. The fact that they were a government section supported by thousands of subordinates that made up an executive arm of a Cyber oligarchy often escaped them.

The room was a storm of debate. One of the spies would raise their voice over all of the others. Then a clamor caught their attention from outside one of the exits. A wailing and sobbing sounded from beyond a curvilinear bookshelf that doubled as a door. Someone was hysterical. And since all twenty-three seats of the circular council were filled, they knew it was not one of their own that had fallen ill.

"Jesus" said Waltz and raked his eyes.

The Round Room was a hidden headquarters made up of circular walls covered in soundproofing foam from floor to ceiling. There were four doors amongst these, and anyone leaving needed to know which codes would unlock the nearest exit, or they were trapped and questioned by the Warriors.

But no one in the Digital Branch department knew exactly where they worked or what they did... just who and what they were... higher ranked individuals with clearance codes for every level and likely, in-the-flesh cyber-warriors. Reverence of the top level spies kept the office running smoothly together, despite the many different employees demarcated place in the Manhattan headquarters of Cyber's Digital Branch.

8

TRIAL AND ERROR

Waltz was closest to the particular exit where the howling emanated from and wanted to get out from under the scrutinizing eyes for a while anyway. He flicked back the safety on his gun, placed it back within his shoulder holster, and lifted the metal shield to the keypad. It was a code of "*Macbeth*", one of his favorites. Seams in the circle showed and the bookcase door floated outward. He squinted as he passed into a corridor of bright white.

The underground engine room was filled with silver air handlers, gray pipes, and humming motors that gleamed in the bright overhead lights. As Waltz's eyes adjusted, he could see the source of the noise clearly: a youth, no more than sixteen, writhed on the cement floor yelling. He held his hands over his head and from his fingers dark blood trickled in thin lines.

The cruel bastards, thought Waltz.

The Cyber Elite had installed booby traps to ensure the commanders' identities remained secret; at least that was what they said. Waltz thought they just wanted to test their would-be future spies in the cruelest ways imaginable. It was bad enough that many would spend their entire lives attempting to hack and force their way forward if they were to ever go so far as making it into the same building as the Digital Branch and the cyber-warrior's ranks.

"I'm sorry, kid. You were caught in a trap" said Waltz. He did his best to remain calm, to try and soothe the youth.

They stood in what was the world's cleanest engine room, but blood stuck to the floor, like syrup. The place was kept spotless by a team of maintenance workers who did not know why they scrubbed the motor room so hard; they would never that it was frequented by others and that the cyber-warriors would not dirty themselves in there upon entering the disguised Round Room. For a long time the youth just sobbed.

"God, what am I going to do?" asked the young man. He sat on his haunches and looked at his stained hands. He might have been fifteen years old. "You're one of them, aren't you?" he said finally. "Are you going to kill me?"

"No. You found us... if you still want to become a cyber-warrior" said Waltz dropping his voice to a whisper.

"Really?"

It was not the cold, wonton process that pissed off Waltz as much as it was the eagerness and desperation that had been created; he heard it in the youth's voice even after they had permanently disabled him. Waltz had wanted to break into the cyber-warriors just as badly, not too long ago that he did not remember that feeling; he had grown up yearning for it with his every breath... but not as much as most. If the very establishment that he had hoped to join were to wrench an eye from him for the sake of a meaningless test, he would have lashed out at them until death parted their ways.

But Waltz had always kept a level of individuality that few had not been bred out of. This youth, however, was lost in the lust for a lifestyle he did not know, could not fathom, let alone understand. Nothing was as secretive as Cyber, except the Cyber Elite themselves. The periphery of what seemed real and what bordered on the shadows made up a never ending and unseen battlefield. Waltz found the motor room emergency comms and called in for a paramedic.

As the nurse whisked away the injured, Waltz turned back to the wall of pipes that doubled as a bookshelf door on the other side. By one of the open valves was a fake scanner. A sharp, silver claw still clutched the youth's eyeball, as strands of blood vessels hung, dripping jelly-like viscous fluid onto the floor.

9

PERSONAL

Three Hours and Ten Minutes Earlier:

The Round Room was an open space crowded with twenty-three individual computer desks arranged in a wide circle facing each other. Antique wood, stainless steel, and glass desks of all shapes, sizes and colors adorned the floor. At each sat an individual as unique as their accompanying workstation. Eleven men sat with all manner of modest or flashy suits, facial hair, and heights. Eleven women sat in an even more diverse fashion as business suits intermingled with modest and spectacular dresses.

One transgender sat there too, as neither man nor woman, in a plain black suit, an indistinguishable white shirt, and black tie. No one knew if Ro was more man or woman, or equally split, and no one cared, because Ro's skills were unparalleled even in a room full of supreme talents.

Of the twenty-three, nine were missing an eye, though seven of these had working robo-placements in the socket that nearly mimicked a real eye perfectly. Only the light catching the robotic irises the right way betrayed Racquel, Connor, Suzie, Geva, Phillipe, Jasmine, and Harrelson by casting a thin rainbow-like reflection, like the sun casts through a magnifying glass. Dedway and Agnetti wore sable eye patches over their right sockets; they resisted putting electronics in their bodies for fear of their being hacked or malfunctioning – it was a common fear in a society that increasingly merged the physiological with the electronic.

From the translucent slab of glass, Waltz had his laptop open, as a large projection blinked on in the middle of the circle. He connected to it with thick wires feeding his computer from a terminal fixed as the back of the desk. The cyber-warriors could look up any amount of information from their own secure networks in that room, their own personal hard lines, and so make so many arguments that it would be impossible to speak audibly without visual aid or fear of being hacked.

"As you can see from the images, the C.E.O. in question turned one individual and one only" said Kingston. "It is probably as simple as a promise of money and power and possibly some exotic reward that could be offered in some remote paradise across the world in Wangluo." He twisted a handlebar mustache obsessively.

"There's more to it" said Waltz. "I knew Doug. He was paranoid, terrified, and refused to go into work the week before he died." He brought up a wrinkled image of fear that had been carved on his friend's dead face.

"So he was frightened at work! Who wouldn't be working for one such as Helena? She had something on him – maybe threatened to unglue his autistic brother. Where's the proof that we haven't plugged the hole in our defense system with their deaths?" asked Geva.

Her accent was hard to place, but thick. She was born in a French-heavy region near Montreal and English was a second language to her; she spoke with a perfect Boston accent when she was in public but let the American fall from her lips whenever she could – it had been decades since Cyber assimilated control of North and South America – but the Canadians still disdained what the United States had been before the Assimilation. Beautiful as Geva normally sounded on that day, she did not even try to hide the contempt in her voice.

"There is no proof, because your vendetta's personal, and it's over."

"It is personal" answered Waltz coldly.

"There's nothing you can say to lessen that point" said Kingston. "In fact, if you ever placed your personal feelings in the group, instead of outside it, in one of our own, then one of us would have long ago dispelled such thoughts from your mind. We will now find and take the cache of deadly arms."

Waltz writhed within; he had not dated since his last partner, Sasha, had died abroad. The order of cyber-warriors took a lifelong oath to only consummate relationships within their Arthurian group – their Round Room reflected their love of the Round Table concept; and carefully bred computing geniuses emerged from such Cyber vows, and the Elite monitored their families closely for future generations of commanders.

"I do want vengeance" said Waltz. "But you're lost on that point... blinded."

"Why do you think the way you do, brother?" asked Ro, referring to him by the ancient term of respect and title that had long been abandoned for curt words that cut to the point harshly. Ro was nearing forty and remembered the early days of Cyber when even a gender outsider (like Ro) was treated with the utmost respect at all times.

"Who gives a damn, hermo?" spat Harrelson harshly.

* * *

Hermo

Noun

Hermo is a derogatory term shortening the word hermaphrodite meaning a person or animal having both male and female sex organs or other sexual characteristics, either abnormally or (in the case of some organisms) as the natural condition.

a plant having stamens and pistils in the same flower.

* * *

Adjective

1. Of or denoting a person, animal, or plant of this kind.

2. Derogatory term of or denoting a transgender human being

* * *

"Where has the respect for the position gone?" queried Ro in disbelief. "Doesn't the President take orders directly from me?"

"You mean the Elite orders the President around, often through you... when they're not licking your ass" said Geva.

"Enough of this bickering! Why would the C.E.O. risk it all for one programmer? Haven't you asked yourselves what Wangluo could be doing with an army of turned programmers and a stockpile of ways to murder millions?" asked Waltz.

"One man, no matter how talented he is, or used to be I should say, is not an army. What would Helena possibly want with an army of programmers, anyway?" asked Agnetti. He grunted softly and scratched deeply beneath his eye patch with a large index finger in what Waltz was sure was an attempt at unnerving everyone in the room.

"How did she get to him?"

"What?"

"You heard me Agnetti" said Waltz.

"On top of your outlandish assumptions, you're still hung up on one traitor's life just because you used to call him a friend?"

"You're missing the point" said Waltz. "He was loyal and Helena got to him. How?"

"Wangluo got to him. Helena was only the messenger."

Keegan Agnetti bellowed in an attempt to squash any support of Waltz being vocalized. Ro and a few of the others had their ears and eyes open and considered Waltz's instincts, while a debate bounded back and forth on the dark hardwood floor. Kingston, Ro, Philippe rose from their charges and spoke within the circle before returning to their desks.

The next minutes pained Waltz's spirit. Some of the strife was on principal, because one would not give in to the other, and some of it was utterly corrupted by individual agenda that all too often directed the actions of those in power. It sickened him. Their strict moral codes seemed hollow when murder was met with such impunity.

His mission outline asked him to wait for confirmation of her location (and that he had taken care of himself). He thanked God that he had gone on his own and gotten to Helena before she could flee and disappear; if she had brought Doug over to Wangluo then anyone in the Round Room could have been their agent.

"Unlike, the citizens of the dictators of the Wangluo government, we are an equal entity – free – and anyone, of any age and creed can join us" said Ro and swirled round and gazed at each in turn.

"Here, here!" said Dedway; he stood and stamped twice in a show of support.

"Not if they have terrorists standing by around the whole damn globe and are set on infiltrating the Round Room at all costs" said Kingston.

He slammed his fist on his desk, and his mustache drooped lower on his bearded chin where it curved up from there. Somehow he ignored the magnificent spurs of facial hair completely and adjusted his square rimmed spectacles. No one knew what color his eyes were, as the lenses were always tinted deep yellow. "A damned bunker just tried to break into this very room, and his purpose was malevolent!"

The sound of a zipper broke the silence. Waltz had had enough. He packed up his laptop in a soft case made from wetsuit rubber. Then he stuffed the secure computer into his brown leather attaché case. Glaring, he patiently joined the two buckles that closed the flap over the old satchel. His silence and patience spoke volumes more than his words could in the room of egos.

That fallen youth had given an eye to be one of them, and he was no bunker, thought Waltz.

A bunker was a nickname given to the CPU runners that controlled and reset the machines from impromptu dug bunkers near to the battlefield. They were fairly talented hackers that had not earned a way out from the frontlines where bombs, robotic tanks, soldiers, and helidrones often shortened their lives; bunkers became very rich and either progressed to become programmers on the virtual battle lines, or grew into grizzled generals that retired once a certain salary had been attained or they were demoted permanently to the army's rotting corpses division. Waltz had been a bunker for a year, at fifteen, and the derogatory use of the term ended the Round Room meeting for him.

10

FLIGHT LATER:

Before he descended the dusty stone steps, Waltz grabbed a lantern dangling from a stake in the wall. He turned on the solar-powered light and prayed that there was enough juice left in the batteries to get him down the three flights safely; he had not left the lantern out in the sun to charge in a couple of months. Spitting, he tore at the webs that stuck to his hair, nose, and lips with his free hand.

"How the hell did they find me?"

The very idea was disconcerting. Each cyber-warrior was given any of a number of different identities to use consistently in various public spheres in order to protect their birth name. In the eyes of most of the Cyber citizens, Waltz was some kind of businessman doing some of the government's marketing – it was public knowledge that they were always recruiting ad guys to hire bunkers and programmers' assistants through Webvision TV and commercials.

The escape route twisted in a spiral staircase three stories down. There was a corresponding fireplace door on the first floor and a false wall with a tub attached in the basement bathroom just below that. He passed these secret passages down to the tunnels.

It has to be one of them... Cyber, he thought angrily. *The slogs!*

He would have yelled to high heaven of the betrayal if it had not meant almost certain death. And whoever they had sent, they were in his house and probably knew every square inch of it down to the architect's schematics. Cyber had access to everything by right. *The sanctity of my fucking home*, he thought morbidly.

The light dimmed. Waltz cursed softly, winced in his lack of restraint, and shook the old LED lantern. The dying device blinked and grew a little brighter before starting to go dark again. He rushed down the last steps and arrived at a tiny stairwell at the bottom where a rough brick wall stood barring entry or exit from the place.

He knocked the lantern's metal cap into the brick, and it lit dully. He found the twenty-third brick up in the twenty-third row and pushed it carefully inward. A thump and a scraping followed. The three hundred year-old brick returned itself to its place and the fulcrum was activated. The entire wall slowly began to revolve.

As the lantern died, Waltz was already through the opening and running hard. He did not need to see. The tunnel was wide enough and high enough for three; the English colonists had carved it from an existing cave in the foothills of northern Long Island – he had looked long and hard for something like it when he was house hunting.

Someone knows me.

Waltz thought he had been careful to hide his tracks whenever he went from home to work. Most of his work he did from a Cyber secured box of an office. His networks were completely contained. None of that security had prevented his personal space from being discovered and violated though.

He hoped the assailants, whoever they were, did not know the secret Waltz had found out when he had first bought the property and built on top of it ten years prior. The tunnel connected a manor that had previously stood on his property to a colonial chapel and then on to a local inn. He tossed the dead lantern and trotted on toward the chapel in the dark.

11

ERROR_

The smartphone had been left behind on the desk. God knew where the computer was. *There's nothing for it*, he thought.

The phone's light was not going to help Waltz through to the chapel. The underground passage was made up of stone and dirt but went straight and level, and he cautiously jogged with a hand held up in front of his chest, blind.

The A-block was a quarter-inch thick piece of solid glass, a half-tablet, half-smartphone rectangle that had been borne out by nanotools and filled with transparent SSD and board sets that were put together like a ship in a bottle. With it he could do close to anything that his primary computing machines could on the phone, albeit at a slower pace. It had been charging when the shots began, and the assailants would soon find it.

They would not see anything useful on his A-block. As soon as the phone was accessed a silent alarm tripped and the user had twenty seconds to enter a code and thumbprint before the entire solid state drive divided itself into ultra-encrypted fragments of files and uploaded them to two secure locations masked as mp3's while the A-block then fried its own SSD beyond recognition. The cellphone essentially transformed itself into a semi-explosive piece of charcoal.

Waltz misjudged the space and nearly knocked his head on the door at the end of the tunnel. He slid his hand down a rough, chalky cast iron surface, a doorknocker, and across carved wood before finding a stiff doorknob. With an effort the knob turned and the heavy door clanked open with a long groan from its ancient hinges.

The dark was still impenetrable but Waltz knew that a narrow staircase rose steeply, and he charged forward seeking an end to his blindness. At the top, out of breath, he came to another door. He knew death could be waiting for him beyond it.

He was unprepared digitally, being bereft of his computers, and physically, since he was a hundred and seventy pounds wet and had not taken his B9 pistol with him. It sat next to the A-block where he had thrown it and the extra clips onto the desk so that he would be free of the weight of them for a while. All that he had, as far as an advantage, was a keen mental capacity and a grudge.

He opened the door and was blinded by white light and the sound of rain tumbling.

12

THE OLD WAYS OF FIGHTING

The Golgotha mural stretched ten feet across on the wall of the ancient chapel's storage room. Waltz had always found it creepy to find the Viking's heroic vision of bloody death enshrined. But that was precisely the point: glorious death.

A storm had picked up. The room was small and had a stale smell of dust and the faint undertone of gunpowder. He sat on a wooden crate and rubbed his bony knees. Lightning flashed and the chandelier flickered above him.

"I admitted it was personal" he mumbled. *Is that it? They had to have known I only said that to make a point. They wouldn't come down on me for that.*

Bits of the Round Room discussion swam inside his head. Thunder shook the wooden walls. He wanted his sarcasm to derail any attempts at labeling him sentimental. And that it had accomplished.

"Maybe they've had enough of my resistance to the new cultural elements" he whispered and thought of the tech implants that many in the North and South Americas now wore in the skull and up into their brain receptors, by choice

There's got to be more than that though. I've earned my way.

The door to the main room in the congregational church lurched open. Soldiers in black traversed the rows of pews, with flashlights attached to their rifle barrels. Narrow beams of light crossed and sliced through the air, this way and that. Waltz heard this and knew in that instant that he had been tracked digitally.

"Dial this" he said, and started to lower the handle on the dynamite detonator. The hand carved doors were works of art, and even though he was not a member of the church it pained him to destroy a longstanding piece of the north shore's history. He had only wired the whaler's dynamite to the foundation as a last resort, knowing that it was locked and empty every day but Sunday and the remaining priests were too blind to notice the trapdoor in the storage room's floor where the detonator had hung for nearly ten years.

The soldiers approached the altar near the back of the church wearily. They knew nothing of the explosives because there was no electric charge or digital timer to light up their thermal scanners; the bomb was crafted the same way it would have been strung together in the 1800's. The occasional flicker of lightning glinted off of bionic eyes and cast an artificial glow. Red flame swallowed their armored bodies whole.

Waltz was already gone as fire engulfed the old church. He retreated from the tabernacle that held the host and holy water and all but fell down the stair as he scattered a bookshelf full of Bibles and then crawled down the tunnel. The secret passage shook for a full minute, grew scarlet and hot, but did not collapse.

He was sad. The wooden church had stood since the 1830's. It had been a relic that held great character, as age made its unique mark over the years. And he had damned it.

Without thinking, two long fingers jabbed at the back of his throat and Waltz threw up his lunch on the rocky floor.

"I knew it."

In the crème colored pool were chunks of pizza and a tiny tracking chip, no larger than a bay leaf and thin enough to be translucent, blinked red in the shadowy underground.

13

XERA

Tara's Inn loomed ahead. The dark redwood archway had been weather stained and aged through at least a hundred years of near perpetual war and black market activity. But that was all that Waltz knew about the place. He had never gone any further than giving it a glance as he passed and went on down Main Street's steep hills.

A fire engine went screaming down the hill, and a few police cars followed. His glance followed them to North Country Road. The teeming flumes of black smoke stretched higher and higher until the wind bent them south toward Waltz, as though the church's soul was following him. He looked back to Main Street.

The area was a business derelict. Places came and went, sometimes refurbishing the faded signs and building fronts, and sometimes leaving them peeling and crumbling in the wind and rain. Despite the incessant flow of people on the busy road and sidewalk, the actual town of Port Jefferson was still half a mile further downhill and north where Main Street ended onto the dock and ferry; that was where the money, and the well-kept colonial port's buildings stood.

The gritty strip along the road near Tara's relied on an overflow of business from the town down Port. Residents, politicians, travelers, tradesmen, and ferrymen helped maintain a healthy profit margin for various lines of trade, including eating, drinking and other discrete establishments.

"Screw it" Waltz said to himself as he crossed the sloping road and pulled open a heavy wooden door. Instead of light pouring out of the doorway, like he had expected, a deeper blackness seeped out to greet him. A cat hissed at him and took a swipe at his pants' leg as he passed within.

He climbed a narrow staircase in the dark. At the top was a single apartment that stood directly above a Hearth King store on the first floor. He had never been there.

The closest contacts he had to friends had long ago begged him to disappear before either Cyber fell, or someone killed him, or both. And the way to safely fade from high society, they all said solemnly, was to go to Xera's with a fistful of cash and favors.

Once again, Waltz found himself checking his pockets for the A-block phone that was not there. He walked slowly to the end of the hall in the dark and felt wholly unprepared. Before his hand could touch the door there was a buzz and someone spoke to him.

"Tell me who you are and why you are here" said a silky voice.

"My name is William Waltz. Is this Xera?"

"Is that why you're here? What do you want with Xera?" she said.

"Yes" he said.

"Yes?"

"Yes, that's why I'm here. I'm not comfortable discussing business with someone from the other side of a door" he said coolly. Shadows draped the hallway and added to his unease. He was not used to being given the third degree before even getting a look at his interviewer or his surroundings. Fear gave way to anger and annoyance. He turned to stalk away.

"Business, Mr. Waltz?" He stopped and rounded back.

"Yes. With Xera. Is there a way I can see about meeting with her?" he asked.

"She is indisposed for the foreseeable future I am afraid, Mr. Waltz" said the voice growing playful and sultry.

"It's important."

"I'm afraid you'll have to come back another"

"I can't! You tell her that a powerful client is going to be dead if she does not intervene right now" said Waltz quickly. "If I seem on edge, it's because I'm not used to being the one that's threatened, but there it is."

"Looks like I'll be able to coax more than one word conversations out of you after all. Last question: where did you hear the name Xera?"

"Smokin' Joe Ricca. He's a bit of a slob, but not a bad guy. I occasionally barter with him in Port" answered Waltz.

"I'm going to buzz you in. I can't get to the door just now, but you can come in and tell me all about your... business" she said. A loud buzz shook plaster dust from the ceiling. He stepped into Xera's and was happy to see that at least one lamp was on.

14

THE WOMAN

Despite a single lamp on an end table, Xera Finn's place was a house of shadows. The deep gray lines and black circles crisscrossed and draped Xera's, keeping the place hidden in every way. Only a bathroom at the far end of the hall offered any real light, and it spilled from the door that was ajar, like sunlight following a lunar eclipse. He squinted and heard rain begin to pelt the roof outside.

In actuality, the light in the bathroom was not that bright. William Waltz entered the doorway and saw that two lampshades, made of thick frosted glass, covered a pair of fifty-watt incandescent bulbs that protruded from each side of the wall behind the sink; he would not have been able to shave in that kind of light.

He stepped fully into the room and stared down at an extraordinary pale woman. She was stretched out in a corroded iron bathtub with one stockinged leg over the rim, while her head rested back on a rolled up towel. Her dark, piercing eyes looked at him in a relaxed, observant manner and her hair hung in wet strands toward the floor, as though it were fingering her very brain. He caught his breath. The other crumpled stocking was coiled about one of a series of copper pipes protruding from the wall next to her white head.

Though there were patches of moist bubbles all over the cracked tile floor, the bubble bath in the tub had all but subsided completely. Her large, round breasts swelled up just over the water level. Her left arm extended straight out on the rim of the antique tub and a white-gloved hand hung in the air, perpendicular to her wrist, and flexed.

It was not her naked body in the blue & green water, but her demeanor and pained gaze that had most of Waltz's attention. The young, sad woman breathed slowly as she looked him over from the rusting tub. She was not the least bit embarrassed or annoyed at his intrusion, just a little troubled that her lone escape from the grime of the world had to be interrupted. And with that gaze, she studied his character like no one had ever done before, with a fixed expression that could have initially been mistaken as vacant.

"My name is Xera Finn" she said.

"Should I get you a towel or something?" he said and half turned around.

"It's not necessary. I try to remember that modesty is in direct opposition to nature."

"How did you buzz me in from here?" asked Waltz. The curiosity beneath her eyes was so strong that his unplanned question popped out of its own accord. She held his eye intently for a minute.

From the water, she raised her right hand and pointed down to a bronze plated intercom and door buzzer button that was on the wall just out of sight. He did not move forward but bent around and looked at the tile wall behind the tub. Thunder boomed.

On the floor below was an open makeup bag with a mobile phone and an old pistol sticking out of it. He had never seen so large a .357 Magnum outside of a screen before, but he recognized it at once. She was less nude than he had first thought.

"I see. Be careful not to electrocute yourself with those" he said with a smile and nod toward the intercom and her phone.

She did not stir. Her dark eyes looked amused. They said *I'll be just fine, big boy.*

The magma colored layer of corrosion on the outer walls of the tub stood out sharply against the grays and blacks that smudged what might once have been soft slate or light blue bathroom tile. The four grimy tub legs were molded hands, their superfluous fingers bent at the iron knuckles into a kneeling position on the floor, while other fingers bent unnaturally and clawed with long nails at pearls the size of baseballs.

"That thing's creepy."

"It's very old, Mr. Waltz. Why do you fear for your life and seek my help? Surely, Mr. Rica told you that there would be no one more dangerous to go to than me" she said quietly.

"He did. He also said you were the only one that could successfully make someone disappear... if the price was right" said Waltz slowly.

"'If the price was right,'" she mused. "You're an honest man." Her voice purred in the warm room. He did not like how she was teeming with confidence at the thought that he needed her for something so urgently.

"You're not used to being in debt to another, are you?" she asked. "You must be higher up the food chain than I would have ever thought possible. What is your business in New York?"

He looked startled.

"Your accent betrays you. Do I assume rightly that you work with Cyber?" she asked.

He trembled at the thought of revealing himself to a complete stranger when he had spent nearly his entire life protecting his caste and his secret occupation at all cost. Xera just lay there soaking in the tarnished vessel unmoved.

"I'm uneasy talking about that" Waltz said at last.

"You're very honest" she said upbeat. "That's a good start, but it's not enough."

Xera picked her head up off of the towel and then rose slowly and with a graceful flourish wrapped it about her hair. She stepped over the side of the tub, picked up her makeup bag, and started to leave the room. He watched her move intently. She paused and turned to speak softly.

"The water is cooling. I never like to bathe in anything but scalding water" she said silkily. "How about you William?"

15

WHAT IS 133T_SP3@K FOR 'TRUST'?

"Follow me" said Xera.

She looked back over her shoulder and motioned with her index finger for Waltz to follow. If he had managed to fool her into thinking that he had remained composed while in the bathroom, all of that illusion fell straight away as he open-mouth goggled at the gleaming curve of her spine and the perfect bubble below her back.

All wariness dissipated at the crossing of the border into her bedroom. Waltz was, after all, a thirty year old in his prime. He had no sooner entered the threshold then Xera had his back up against the wall and gunmetal in his mouth.

"You're not used to this either, are you?" she asked savagely. The change that had come over her was remarkable.

The anger erupting in his eyes was the only answer she received, and what looked like a heavy brick of slate was pressed to his temple. He did not know why, but that worried him more than the gun did, and he started to shift.

"Hold still. This is a necessary precaution, Mr. Waltz. If you still want to treat with me that is" said Xera.

He nodded impotently in acquiescence; the barrel limited the motion. The cold piece of carbon pressed to his forehead, his neck and on, tracing his entire body, down to his toes. The gun was taken out of his mouth, but not holstered. The gray curvilinear rectangle disappeared in her makeup bag.

“You’re clean” said Xera, letting go of him

“I just checked you for add-ons” she said in response to his furrowed brow.

“Add-ons?”

“Tech, as you know damn well. You’re no amateur. You’re a purist, like me. We believe in keeping the body natural, without robotic add-ons, like a bionic gazer in the eye socket or an adrenal booster in the spinal column, or a hidden router chipset placed directly in the skull. You could even have had a B9 scatter pistol embedded in your forearm, Waltz. I’ve seen it all before.”

“And what would that thing have done to me if I had any tech on me?” he asked sternly. The woman was awfully young to have seen it all before but he needed to know more.

“It’s a magnet... and most of the time... it’s quite harmless” she said with a wry smile. “We would have heard a soft pop, and any phones in your pockets, or electronics in your body would be -for lack of a better word- fried.”

Xera motioned for him to wait outside. Waltz walked into the living room and found a light switch. A tall lamp of an old train engineer with a stopwatch drove out the shadows in the cluttered room. Bookcases stretched up the vaulted ceiling and lined nearly every wall with narrow library ladders attached to metal tracks. There were no TV’s or screens of any kind in sight. He threw up his hands and turned back to the bedroom door.

“And if there were electronics in my brain or spine when you magnetized me?”

"Then you would not be so unscathed, I'm afraid" said Xera levelly. She emerged from the bedroom wearing blue jeans and sharp pointed black boots.

"But I didn't think you were dumb enough to have anything – a phone maybe, but nothing more than that – on your person when you came to see me. This" she said holding up her square makeup bag with the rectangle in it, "is a powerful magnet, and highly illegal. You might have been made into a vegetable."

She shrugged and pulled a black blouse over her head. "In my trade, I can't afford to risk it."

"A little paranoid, aren't we?"

"Have you ever had someone so intent on tracking your movements that they planted nano-trackers into their blood unknowingly?"

"What?"

"My magnet boiled one of my closest friends alive not two years ago."

"Jesus" whispered Waltz.

"What kind of trouble did you get yourself into, Mr. Waltz? You're a top agent of Cyber, a warrior most likely, and yet I'm supposed to believe you when you say that you fear for your life? You don't strike me, as you stand here, as the kind of person that runs away from anything."

"You don't know me very well yet" said Waltz.

A crack of thunder shook the apartment. Xera took a cowhide gun belt from her coffee table and strapped it over her blue jeans. The long pistol disappeared in the leather holster.

"Enough with the pleasantries. I do not play games. Tell me why you're here right now, William Waltz" said Xera, "if you do not want to get shot in the face."

16

SIGHTING

"That was smart thinking, throwing up like that. Especially before you came to see me" Xera said after Waltz had told his tale of the previous twenty-four hours to her. She had listened silently and remained impassive throughout, while he had grown grave.

"If I hadn't, my stomach or intestines would likely have exploded in my body" he said. "Do you even feel the least bit bad about that?"

"No. And if I hadn't magnetized you, I could've been in their custody by now."

"Whose custody?" he asked.

"Whoever is chasing you down – I do not need to know who that is to make you disappear" she replied. "In fact, it would be extremely dangerous for me to do" She broke off.

"Motherfucker!"

Xera turned and rushed to the window. She stared out intently at the view overlooking the sidewalk bazaar, despite the heavy rain and darkness. She grasped for a small pair of rudimentary binoculars, found them, and scanned the crowd by the light of the streetlamp. There was little to discern from the small light reflected in the downpour, but she had marked an unwanted person down there.

17

THE DEAD

Waltz joined her and looked out onto those massed together as far as he could see along the wet road. His eyes strayed left and right where an enormous set of glass panes took up most of the living room wall facing out onto Main Street to make up for the lack of windows in the opposite wall. He could tell that the windows, like the padded antique armchair, coffee table, and fanciful artwork in the apartment, matched her expensive taste for living. It was cunning: she hid herself in a derelict community where the building's hallway where she lived smelt of garbage.

Vulnerability appeared in Xera's armored aura for the first time (that Waltz had experienced), as her eyes went to the window. Someone had rattled her staunch attention and shook her reserve to its core. Waltz was completely forgotten.

"I am prepared to do exactly as you instruct" he said after feigning a cough.

Her slight figure shook violently as if she was startled from a deep sleep. She looked him up and down and calculated.

* * *

"What is it?" asked Xera. She put her arm around the curve of the lower back that was lying next to her on the bed. The fire spit and crackled in the bedroom.

"Why can't you tell me what you do? For work, I mean" said Kailey. She was pretty and just getting into her mid-twenties where curiosity of the world met with experience for a certain measure of wisdom. Xera let her go on.

"I see men come up here, sometimes. From the bar" Kailey said. "I don't care or anything about that – I know you don't care for them – your clients – they just want to be whipped and held down, and you give them that."

With startling speed, Xera reached beneath her pillow and sent out a black leather thong that smacked right across Kailey's ass cheeks.

"Ah!"

"Getting jealous, are we?" asked Xera. "You know I do what I have to... to make a living, love."

"But it can't be all that you do for money" said Kailey sitting up. "Sometimes there are no men or women here for weeks at a time."

"I haven't said more to you, because I didn't want to involve you in this, Kailey. Is it that important to you?"

"It is."

"Okay"

* * *

"You admit to being a cyber-warrior, Mr. Waltz?"

"Yes" he said softly.

"Have you ever been to the market below or Tara's Inn?" she asked. Her eyes had become hard.

"No. I always avoided the place. I live within five miles of here, oddly enough."

Those glass eyes seemed to bore and pilfer into his brain and memory. If Xera was as high up the food chain as she appeared to be, then he felt she should have been able to read his honesty; that was unless she was having trouble reading him altogether.

"Then I can help you" she said finally. Her eyes strayed back to the window where the sidewalk disappeared in the rainy darkness and climbed up to the oak doors of Tara's Inn. "But you must do exactly as I say, and I'll need a down payment for my services that begins now." She pointed below. "There."

18

TARA'S INN

With a welcome nod, Xera was let in. Waltz pushed his way through patrons in line crowding – and clearly thirsty – to get past the bouncer. Waltz's identification was checked, handed back to him with a stern look and he was thumbed in. People of all ages were busy talking, laughing, and cheering sports games projected on the tops of the walls, and everyone had a mug or glass of some kind in their hands. A jukebox belched blues rock loudly into the humid, late night air.

Tara's was a bit strange. Waltz shuffled his way past an oddly placed pool table that seemed to separate the watering hole into two halves a couple of merry bikers in leather vests held their cues up impatiently.

Beyond them he could not help but notice a local Congressman, Arnie Blackwald, leaning on a beat up Formica table in the far corner of the room. The stout Senator wore a loosened pink tie thrown over one shoulder and lectured a crowd of ten eager listeners to be wary of the opposing party's guile. And in Waltz's mind, he knew that all of the political parties were merely stenographers inscribing on paper whatever the Cyber Elite needed to make into public law. The illusion of a political dichotomy kept the public's energy divided. *Hard to believe it all still works*, he thought.

Xera found them a tiny two-person table (that was recently vacated) on one side of the horseshoe layout. Every stool on the bar was taken, and thirsty friends of all shapes and sizes clustered around them. Waltz sat down, smoothed his shirt, and tugged on each of his cuffs as he took in the bustling surroundings. No one paid him any mind.

"Do you see him?" Waltz whispered. She took a long look around and gave him the slightest hint of a nod. He followed her eyes to another two-person table crammed up against an emergency exit door. It was on the opposite end of the room from where Arnie the Congressman instructed his pupils on the *other side's* rampant sexual misconduct with regards to their pages.

There sat a skinny wisp of a man who could not have been much older than thirty. Waltz became unsure of that almost immediately though. The skinny man was an enigma. His face looked far younger than twenty-five at a quick glance, but there were strained veins at the corner of his sunken blue eyes and his long blond hair was mangy and matted in places from years of neglect. What was clear was that he was an addict. And the guy plainly terrified Xera.

"What can I get you, honey?" a young waitress in an emerald Tara's T-shirt asked Waltz. He tried not to let the feeling of surprise show. While Waltz thought for a second, the waitress pulled at the jeans rolled up to her knees.

"You have Guinness here?"

"The best" she said with a broad smile "at least west of Dublin anyways."

"I'll have a pint and a burger with fries" said Waltz. *What could a blond lush like that possibly do to scare Xera?* he thought.

"Big basket or small?"

"How much are they?

"The big basket is $2.50, the—"

"Big, please. I'm starving."

"If the fries cost twenty bucks would you have gotten the small instead?" Xera asked. Her smile broadened into a grin.

"Why does it matter?" The smile disappeared.

"Because I know you. No one in your position would ever have to worry about money" she said.

"It's the principle of the thing."

She knew then that Waltz had not come from a rich or a powerful family, like most who were raised in perpetual training to achieve cyber-warrior status and incessantly aspired to become one of the Elite while they chewed on silver spoons. Rising up out of your Cyber caste was miraculous, and he had done it. Of that she was sure.

"Would you have bought twenty dollar fries if you were really hungry?"

"Nope."

Without being obvious, Waltz pretended to take in a TV image near the ceiling and stared at the addict in the corner. The man scratched at his wrists with filthy black fingernails. Something about him was familiar. The addict stirred from his slouch and looked over in their direction; Xera had already been turned with her back to him, but Waltz had to feign a sneeze into a napkin to avoid the addict's eyes. The dirty white man was more perceptive than he seemed at first glance.

Waltz turned around. He needed to find a local to speak with in view of the addict. All types of folk were said to convene under the roof of Tara's, but he had always avoided the area. The chimney store, the Lobster House, and the pub, were well known black markets, and his job required him to remain clandestine. But the situation had changed, and he needed to make some kind of illegal deal where the observant audience would see him and give him instant credibility in the eyes of the newcomer.

Despite the danger of sitting in with smugglers and criminals, the old Irish look of Tara's resonated with him. The waitress dropped off a frothy black brew and a multicolored Long Island Iced Tea for Xera. The beer was cold. After such a shitty day, it sat right. A plastic plate of steaming hot two-dollar French fries sat even better. He wished he could have stayed there eating fries forever.

The addict continued to sit quite still. His pencil-thin mustache twitched. Either he had communications embedded in his head, or he was even more fun than Waltz had realized.

Waltz noticed that he mumbled softly and select words – Co-jack and Sweet Tooth - got past the ringing in his ears while the loud, automated DJ shut up to change tracks. *The worst kind of synthetic crystal meth offshoots*, he thought morbidly and continued to scan the crowd for someone he could approach with an abnormal request.

A loud clinking stopped him. She looked to the back near the Congressman's table, the kitchen, and the bathrooms. Two antique arcade games and one archaic pinball machine blinked. Their enticing screens glinted brightly with movement in the dim place. The Twentieth Century coin-ops had vintage slots for a quarter that dropped in to allow you to play. They were a game he was familiar with; this was not. He needed to know more.

"What could you possibly want with a junkie like that?" Waltz asked quietly. Xera tore her head from the games and fixed it on him. A twinge of pain and anger tightened her lips.

"He shouldn't be here" she said and took a deep breath. Keeping cool had become difficult for her, despite her training. “He was warned not to come back to Tara’s. Most of the jack’s that come here”

“Wait, what ‘jack’?” he asked.

“A local dealer in Port, and yes, there are enough of ‘em here locally to warrant getting their own label.” He raised his eyebrows.

“The owner of Tara’s does not hold with drugs, William. You can buy a harvested kidney in here, with his leave, and if it’s to save a life he’ll even give you his blessing, but the minute you start dealing in addictive chemicals, of any kind, you get your ass kicked, and you get banned.”

“That bastard over there, his name is Nick Reno. I need you to kill him” Xera added.

A note of barely concealed fury permeated her whispered word and puzzled Waltz. He had the unfortunate experience of having ended human lives before, but it had always been in situations that he was morally and philosophically good with. The dead faces rarely came to visit him in his sleep. But not knowing this man, Nick Reno, made it a different situation altogether.

“Why?” asked Waltz. An old Johnny Cash song echoed deeply in the old room. Some cheered the Man in Black on.

“Reno is a leading tester for the biggest drug cartels on the east coast. He’s an addict, a dealer. He’s also smart as hell. A real psychopath with a freakish resistance to the degradation the drugs should be doing to him physically” she said and her voice was a barely audible trace in his ear.

“He gets a steady supply of his own uncut chemicals and cash, and he just won’t die, no matter the quality or lethality of what he tests for his employers. Many of the most ruthless jacks depend on him to cut up their supply personally before it goes out to the poor souls that buy the shit. He is a bastard" said Xera with her voice raising and trembling slightly.

"He delivered a hot dose to the owner's daughter here, and she... she was a very close friend of mine and not used to taking drugs of any kind." Her head hung low in memory of her deceased girlfriend.

"I'm sorry" he said. "But I find this hard to believe and if I had to guess, I'd say you're a well-placed spy, a cyber-warrior most likely, but not with us. You work for another government, you live a modest lifestyle on the fringe of the black market to hide yourself, and forgive me for being skeptical, but you have the luxury of having friends?"

Though his gut said Xera was trustworthy, Waltz had begun to doubt what she was saying. To be a cyber-warrior was to be alone. That was the nature of the metaphoric beast and it was the first rule of the position. Nothing else could keep you safe in a volatile world of helidrones and miniature camou-bots on every street corner that discerned individual faces and pointed them out to satellite trackers. She knew his secret and could sell him out if it helped her accomplish her revenge; knowing the inner workings of the cyber-warriors would be invaluable and could cripple the regime.

19

RENO

"I won't comment on your shrewd guess. I have quite a few friends, and they're not a liability. What have you gained from being so careful with your alias? You've never made any real friends, have you? If there was anyone that could have helped you out of this mess, you wouldn't have come to me. You've been loyal to your Cyber brethren and played a careful game, I can respect that, but misplaced nationalism hasn't done you any good in the end now, has it?" she asked.

"No, I guess it hasn't. Be straight up with me, Xera. Why do you need me to kill this guy, Reno? You're a capable human being with assets. Why don't you take care of this jack yourself?"

She looked around to see who might be listening. The signal jammers resided in every tin napkin holder on every table, but that did not mute the sound waves that traveled to physical ears and some of those in the room might even have an electronic amplifier to pick up sound. It was part of the reason Tara's never turned the blaring jukebox off when the pub was open. Privacy was paramount for conducting business.

"Nick Reno was escorted from this very room two weeks ago. He had been caught handing over a soda can that was actually lined on the inside with Co-jack" Xera whispered and leaned closer to Waltz "Everyone knew he was a jack but he had never dealt his super amphetamine in Tara's."

"When Reno was caught, he threatened the bouncers, told them all about who he was 'connected' with, and the owner made an appearance and personally banned

Reno for life anyway. Kicked him out" said Xera choking back a sob.

"She got hurt for it, and she wasn't even there." Her voice was hoarse and trailed off. "She never hurt anyone, never had anything to do with the black market, the underworld. She just helped her father run an honest establishment for the thirsty and hungry."

"Two days after Reno's warning, a fisherman found Kailey's body just off the pier in Port, lying with the boulders; she had accidentally overdosed on drugs she never would have taken. And today of all days, Nick Reno just decides to march down the road and enter the scene of the crime?"

"He's sitting there with a smirk, high as a kite, knowing full well that he's visible on every camera in the place. Something's firing in that pisspot he calls a brain. I need you to find out what he knows... before you kill him."

"I don't trust myself. I can't bring myself to do it. I'd lose it and kill him long before finding out what he's set in motion here" said Xera grinding her teeth. "And this is my home. He wants it, and I want him to go fuck himself."

"I don't know" said Waltz. "A blind man can see that he's an addict, is a long time abuser. This is what I'm thinking: I'll bullshit a deal with a smuggler where Reno can see me to gain enough street cred where I'd be able to approach him without getting his back up. Does he know you?"

"Not as you see me now" she said.

"Uh okay" said Waltz. "Interesting."

20

HEART

There was a gleam in the biker's eye that was accentuated by a twitch. Waltz found it unnerving. He sat on the stool next to the pool table and looked around at the stained and beer-soaked oak bar. He looked at the filthy foot rail below and the dusty ceiling... anywhere but in the biker's gnarled face.

"This code magnet is not industry standard" Waltz said quietly raising it to the biker.

"Yeah, but which industry?" he asked. He laughed revealing extraordinarily straight teeth outlined with black tobacco tar. He flexed arms that could have easily hidden Waltz's head behind their circumference.

"The top, chief, it comes from the top of the food chain. I can't say anymore without holding, in my hand" said Waltz as he lowered his voice further, "a fully functional heart frozen in liquid nitrogen at a hundred percent function."

"There's only one way to transport one like that and keep it at a hundred percent" said the burly man. He kicked at a leather saddlebag at his feet. There was a clinking of metal canisters. "I can deliver right here and right now." He stroked his long gray beard, winking, and looked the former cyber-warrior up and down.

"Good."

"My guess is you've got the tech here with you, since you're in such a hurry. What's to stop me from twisting your scrawny neck into a pretzel out back and making off with your head?" asked the biker. He took a long pull from his mug of beer.

"There are two reasons: one is that my partner would have shot you and your friend's thumbs off for trying to strong arm me, and the second is that my scrawny ass would have no trouble twisting you into a pretzel, despite your thickness" said Waltz. "I've been in my share of fights, and I'm not in the habit of letting people walk away from me." He could not have been calmer or more direct.

"You're a funny man." The biker's eye twitched for a full ten seconds.

"A sense of humor is a prerequisite where I work."

"Now quit blinking or I'm going to pluck your eye from your skull right now." Waltz held up his index and middle fingers together. "Nothing gets past a cyber-warrior."

The biker choked on his brew and it spilled down his neck. The claim and the fact that Waltz was reckless enough to make it out in full view of the public, in front of many cameras and who knew how many microphones, terrified the biker.

"Jesus man, I didn't know. How could I? Do you still want to do this? We can trade right now, if you want.

Waltz measured the biker carefully and then looked over at his vested pool partner who was playing eight ball with himself. He could either make the fair trade, give the biker the tool – an invaluable one that he would never be able to get again from Cyber headquarters – or he could screw the guy for threatening him publicly.

"Here's how we're going to do this" said Waltz at a whisper. "Your insult didn't sit right. So hand me over the heart, and I let you live, no strings attached."

To the amazement of the biker's partner, who missed his next shot completely, the burly man scratched his beard, grunted, and handed over the heavy satchel. His eyes did not blink at all. Waltz could feel the cold through the heart's casing and the thick leather. He purposefully looked everywhere in Tara's, pretending to care for the organ's safety, except where Nick sat; Xera had caught his curious glance take in the heart transaction.

As Waltz sat back down at the table, he searched many eyes and found the jack's. Nick Reno nodded. A fully functional heart was useful when cocaine and poppy products frequently decayed, clogged, and overrode the existing pumps. Genetics, cell replication, and the advent of the 3D printer had brought about unique custom-fitted organs partially printed and partially grown to match a recipient's exact DNA. The replicant organs were miracles of medical science for those wealthy enough to be able to afford them. Universities all over the United States had purchased most of the patents pertaining to the genes and replicant therapy and relied on private corporations for funds in exchange for rights to sell replicant hearts, lungs, legs, eyes, and even brain tissue, though that was a new and unproven field.

21

A TALK

A real heart dipped in gene therapy would be worth a lot to our clients and beat the hell out of what the Chinks were printing over in China, the addict thought.

Nick dragged his chair over to Xera and Waltz's table. She got up and went to the bathroom. He stared at the matted hair and stained t-shirt and waited for the addict to make the first move. He stank of body decay.

The process of growing organs on printed templates and retrofitting them to a person's unique DNA system was a huge industry in Japan and Singapore, because of the much lower costs on the black market – a heart often went for the equivalent of fifty thousand dollars – but it was very unstable. The risky organ imports often resulted in the recipient becoming very sick over months as their cells did battle with each other and either incapacitated or killed them. This was a well-known result of the rejected replicant organ going off like a time bomb, but people still grew desperate enough to try their luck.

"I don't know what you said to old Jonah, but his head lost three different shades of color" said Nick. "The guy's face practically matches the green felt on the pool table" he said with a hoarse laugh.

"Wouldn't you like to know" said Waltz coolly. The addict laughed shrilly and coughed. His voice broke and cracked with each word and grated on the cyber-warrior's nerves. "I'm told you want a heart."

"Among many other things" said Nick. "What are you looking to get out of it?

The two heads lowered together, conspiringly, and Waltz lowered his voice. "I want a kilo of uncut H tonight.

"Is that all?" asked Nick with a short laugh. He itched a raised seam along the outline of an Ace tattoo on his forearm. "No one sells uncut H."

"You do. No one sells harvested hearts that are ready to be installed. Stop dicking around. Do we have a deal?"

"I'll have to find an unstretched supply and bring it back here. Can you meet me in the back alley in fifteen, fifteen, fifteen minutes?" asked the addict.

"I'll be there, just know that if you try to fuck me" said Waltz, "you'll die a slow death."

"Make sure you're alone."

22

TAKING A SHOT

The narrow alley behind Tara's Inn consisted of a loading dock and cement walls. Alongside the market next door, wooden crates littered black pavement that sloped steeply downhill and provided a few parking spots for patrons that wished to avoid being noticed on the main road. It was frequently full of cars. As discreet and abandoned as the area was, even the homeless avoided the alley for fear of waking to find that their organs had been harvested while they slept off their troubles, just like the owner's daughter had been found... overdosed and empty.

When Waltz stepped out back behind Tara's Inn, he was alone and soaked. Nick Reno was already there; he lifted a two-inch long pinky fingernail to his nose and inhaled a perfectly measured line of Sweet Tooth. He breathed deeply in three times from the yellow server and looked up slowly. He did not seem to notice the rain pouring onto his face.

"Have a seat" said Nick with a flourish. The collar of his jacket was flipped up and much of his lank hair was hidden within it. He gestured with the putrid fingernail to a crate beside him.

"What are you doing?" asked Waltz quickly. "I don't want to go to jail today." He was not really afraid, but he felt it wise to play Nick Reno as well as he could.

"You won't" said the grating voice. "The owner's already on a plane to Los Angeles, and he's left me the keys and the deed. There ain't no one going to call the cops on us."

"There's no way"

"Something about the man's daughter and being too close to the tragedy and all. He left this all to me for a small sum" said Reno. He gestured to the building behind him and shrugged at his good fortune. Waltz laughed.

"There's no way in hell he'd deal with you. Not after what you did."

"So you know?" he asked. The addict acted as though he had just scored a point and was clearly playing his new client to learn what he knew.

"Okay then... I had some friends remove the guy from here about an hour ago and fit him with custom tailored cement shoes" said Reno. "I'm sure they'll fit him comfortably. Now, if you don't want to end up like that little lady organ donor friend of yours, I'd suggest you hand over the heart right now, friend." Nick beckoned eagerly to Waltz with his filthy right hand and the sharpened fingernail stuck out almost as unnaturally as his open mouthed smile.

Waltz was about to say that she was no friend of his, but never got the chance.

A dark dot appeared on the addict's palm. The rain mingled with the dirty puddle and then another bigger crimson drop splashed down.

"Shit!" said Nick. He lowered his bleeding nose to his sleeve, and there was a crack behind his head. A bit of the building's brick tumbled out. Without thinking, Waltz pulled Reno down to the ground. A gun fired twice more.

With surprising agility and speed, Reno rolled himself forward into a ball to get behind a Volkswagen Beetle nearby as a few more bullets pierced the wall where he had been seated. Waltz rose to a crouch and rushed behind the nearest car as three more shots thundered. Then all was quiet for a minute.

"Well I'll be damned. The Mayor's never failed me before" said Nick. He cautiously looked out and then straightened. "You've got some great reflexes there, friend. I could use a guy like you. What do you say?"

Another crack sounded and a bullet made a hole in the hood of the Beetle that Nick stood behind dumbly. Waltz pulled Reno down a second time just a split second before another round nearly took his head off. He flushed with fear and started shaking his head from side to side counting, "One, two, three. One, two, three." Reno was high and he was afraid.

Unfortunately for Waltz, his association with the addict made him a target as well. He punched in a message and ducked lower.

"You thought a couple of goons would be enough to take me out?" said a deep voice calling down from the roof of the building. His Irish accent was thick.

"You may have been able to overpower my lass, but she was young "he said. "I'm old and tough as a pesky tree root that won't die no matter how much you cut at it with an ax."

"How?"

"I sank in the Sound with a small hammer in my pocket and I broke away the cement just in time, you fuck. And am I glad my front door was loose. Drown this, motherfucker!"

A sound like a nail gun stuck on fire mode flew overhead and the owner of Tara's, who had named the old pub after his dead wife, unloaded an automatic weapon. Glass and debris flew through the lines of rain and fell amongst Waltz and Reno as they sat covering their heads. Blood covered the addict's face and jacket.

A concentrated shot of light, like a beam of lightning lit up the entire alley and temporarily blinded the owner. He stopped firing and Xera threw a smoke grenade up onto the roof. After a cough and a curse the owner fled. He would make sure Nick Reno died, even if he had to flee from the unexpected firepower of Reno's friends and regroup. Patience would only heat up the vengeful blood boiling in his veins.

Xera climbed up a fire escape to the rooftop, but soon lost track of the owner – the would-be assassin–. She returned and found Waltz squatting behind the car and looking around wearily. The addict continued to fearfully turn his head left and right in fear and count, "one, two, three. One, two, three."

"Stop counting, Reno."

"If I stop counting all of our heads will EXPLODE!" he screamed. "One, two, three. One, two, three."

"Jesus" said Waltz.

23

REVENGE

After a couple of long minutes waiting, Reno stopped shaking and counting. He sniffled and dabbed at the dried, crusty blood under his nose. He took a plastic vial from a hidden pocket and carefully tilted it, filling his fingernail with a golden powder. The contents were snorted in three sweeps of his nose. Blood began to flow again, as his eyes rolled back.

"Under the circumstances" said Waltz wiping rain from his eyelids, "do you think you should be doing that?"

Nick grinned with pleasure; blood covered his teeth.

"Do you recognize me?" asked Xera. His smile faltered.

Curiosity and doubt overruled the fear. Reno was confused. He swept aside the matted hair that screened his dilated eyes to get a good look at Xera's face. He scrunched his splotchy face in a state of deep thought.

"Are you a customer of mine? A happy one, I hope?"

"Yes" she said quietly "a happy one."

24

GOING BACK HOME

The alert had come in from her assistant, Irene. This isn't good, thought Xera. Fuck. And I'll have to let Reno go too... for now. This isn't good.

It was not good. She had just asked Irene, her body's part-time pillager, to prepare her masseuse table when the headline came in on the news feed and tore at the ulcers lining her digestive tract.

Irene said that the ID scan was confirmed; Waltz had stared at Xera's naked ass in her bathtub long enough that the room's retinal scans had completed their work. He was who he said he was, which was the good news. The bad news was that she was no nearer to knowing what division of Cyber or what location he actually worked in. He had no record anywhere and no known associates. Someone had all but erased him from history already.

She just knew where they stood. And it was not good at all.

25

RAW DEAL

How do I break this to him? Xera wondered. *If he runs, I'll have no choice.*

"Take the heart and go" she said coldly. Waltz started to shake his head at her, but an angry look stopped his protest abruptly. Reno reached out his chalky palms to take the case, and she thought they looked like the hands of a filthy skeleton covered in sweat.

As he grasped a hold of the case, Xera put a hand on it stopping him. Reno handed a wad of bills to her.

"We want more credit, Nick. You understand? Things are too hot right now, wouldn't you agree? We can deal again later?"

"Yes, yes, yes. Of course. I shall remember your face now" he said. "Here's my number."

And as he looked long and hard at Xera's face, she activated the tracker clip, which was the size of a staple and fastened to the outside of the heart's casing the same way a stapler would bind pages together. Waltz saw this swift action while the two had a staring contest that sealed their deal just like a handshake would in the legitimate business world.

No sooner had Nick Reno disappeared into the distant fog then Xera turned her scatter pistol on Waltz. The rain streaked along the black shine of the barrel. Without thinking, his legs started to bend and squat, like a frog preparing to leap away.

But then he changed his mind. He trusted her – at least in some small way – and evasion disappeared from his mind and his muscles. He took a deep breath, relaxed, and raised his hands and acquiesced.

26

REVELATION

"An alert's been put out over the airwaves, Waltz" she said before he had a chance to ask what she was doing pointing a gun at his chest instead of working to protect and hide him.

"What kind of an alert?"

"The worst kind: you've been named publically as a traitor and defector, operating as a spy. You're considered armed and dangerous and you're wanted dead or alive." Xera continued to study him as though seeing him for the first time.

"But that's to be expected isn't it?" asked Waltz in his deep, quiet voice. "They're flushing me out. I am paying you to help me get out of this, and I have a lot of money or favors to make it worth your while to deliver for me.

Yes, overseas. He's determined and obstinate, thought Xera. *He really thinks that he'll beat the rap.*

"Thing is, the Elite's press people are framing it like you're working as a cyber-warrior for the East, and I know you haven't joined our cause" said Xera, "because I'm a cyber-warrior from the East."

27

JACKED

The two of them stood there looking at one another in the freezing rain for a long time. The loading dock stank and the pale light just outside the alley made them both nervous, as Tara's patrons continued to walk up and down the sidewalk oblivious to the shooting that had just taken place minutes earlier. The Port's black market had known some disagreements to be argued out with firepower before and it would again.

"There's only one way I can see you beating this now that you're hidden identity is public knowledge. They'll have heard about this in Shanghai by now, William. You'd have to find out exactly who, on the inside of your cyber-warrior circle, set you up and you'd have to turn this on them in a way that the world would believe that they were the traitors and you were not who they said you were" she said and pulled up her right bra strap nervously. Her gun did not waver.

"I have to break deep into Cyber to do that" he thought aloud. "Can you lower that please?" he said pointing to the weapon in her slender hand.

"I need assurance you won't try and run on me" she said.

"What?" Waltz could not hide the surprise that clogged his throat.

"The jack and others saw us together tonight. And if you run and are caught my life will be over." The rain picked up and with its ferocity seemed to crowd in closer to them in the night.

"I won't get caught."

"I can't take that chance. Before the alert was made public, I could've erased your ID easily enough; I can't get you through weeks of gene therapy and plastic surgery now, someone would find and kill you before we could ever leave New York. No, there are only two ways that will insure that I won't be compromised: one is that you die and I bury you deep"

"And the other?" he asked feigning mirth.

"You track down who did this to you, and we flip it around, turn the tables on them. Now" she said getting a strange curl to her mouth that must have been her tight-lipped attempt at a grim frown "give me a good reason not to kill you."

"M.J." whispered Waltz.

"What?"

"I have one friend, my friend's brother actually – Jordan – and he's deep on the inside of Cyber. He's not in as deep as I need, but he might be talented enough to make up for that in spades" he said brightening at the thought. The shining black barrel of Xera's gun was lowered slowly.

28

JORDAN

Jordan choked in anguish as he forced the mechanized IV into the bulging vessel in his left forearm. His stomach muscles were taught and his breathing came in gasps, as he pushed the wide needle painfully deeper, inch by inch.

"Jesus!" he cried and threw his head back to look away.

The pain was excruciating but what was worse was the feeling of the foreign object clawing its way into his skin further and further into the very depths of his sacrosanct body. The blood vessel accepted the unusual instrument, *thank God*, thought M.J. There were rumors on the black market that some body's rejected the Receptacles as they went in and those unfortunate souls had died clutching their open arms while the IV squirmed and clutched and tried to force its way back into the bleeding vein.

The Receptacle IV was far longer than any known medical device and it widened to a sterile microbot designed as a spider on the end of a hollow stick. It crawled and pushed deeper and deeper into his swelling vein. Sweat fell and mingled with the tears being squeezed from the corner of his eyes.

"Jesus!"

The semi-autonomous receptacle spider assisted in pushing the IV further in than would be comfortable for anyone self-inserting such a device (and with their illegality most did install it themselves); once the spider was satisfied it clamped down in the arm, immobilizing the entire IV.

God, what if I ever need to take it out, thought M.J. I never bothered to ask about taking it out. Would it even let me? Had anyone ever managed it before?

The spider pushed until he screamed. It needed every effort of will not to try and tear the entire thing from his forearm. The brain of the Receptacle IV and the micro chipset were near the top of the spider's head and was the only part visible on Jordan's arm as it finally ceased moving. Jordan's entire side throbbed but at least it was fairly still and only his own shakes and voluntary movements stirred.

He could not relax though, not yet. *Please be clean, please be clean, please be clean, oh God,* thought M.J.

Using his right arm only, careful not to budge the left, Jordan fumbled to pluck the cloudy plastic cap from a small syringe's top. The cap flew up and then clacked to the floor, ignored. With the bare needle, Jordan plunged the tester into his thigh and drew some blood. He winced in pain.

A red cloud formed in the translucent belly of the syringe tester and began to blink with a neon blue LED light. Acquiring a sterile Receptacle had cost him nearly everything he had, but that did not mean that the seller had not pulled one over on him. The frosty color flashed for thirty seconds and then the whole cylinder went neon green.

"Thank you, oh God, thank you" M.J. said. "There are no worms."

For the first time since he had begun over an hour earlier, Jordan felt a sense of relief soak his brain and wash over his body. He had accomplished what he had set out to do: a rectangular female connection, like a dark gray gunmetal port for a music player protruded from his skin; silvery teeth were visible as they ran around the entire inside of the Receptacle's mouth; his own body's electricity could now be used in conjunction with myriad bits of software, some organic and some inorganic, and he could plug in.

The newest, most versatile, and most dangerous form of cyber tech was his. Anyone reliant on wireless tech dealt with slower, inefficient mechanisms that could not compare to a Receptacle. For all intents and purposes it was invisible. He would break into the cyber-warrior echelon. He could plug in.

29

THE MINERS

The miners returned and simultaneously spurred the economy and wreaked havoc wherever they landed. Sheetrock – his friends called him that because they had never really remembered how to say his full name, Benjamin Sheetreich – and his crew fell from the sky at a rate of speed approaching Mach Two. The afterburners lit, the resistance panels opened, and the subsequent opposing force of heated air slowed the ship enough to prevent it from burning and breaking up in the atmosphere. The Thanos, the S.S.S., short for submersible space shuttle, instead slowed and skidded along a neon-lit runway on the Long Island Sound before it came to a stop and floated on the rocky water half a click from Port Jefferson.

Under his breath, Sheetrock uttered thanks to the Gods of space and sea for his safe return, and then he barked orders at the five uniquely odd members of his crew. He blinked as their shadows emerged in the bright light of the hatch.

The job required long months of isolation in deep space and the asteroid mines they drilled out and manned were among the most dangerous working conditions that could be undertaken by humankind. Robots had been tried at the trade by dozens of companies for years, but no bot or semi-autonomous drill could ever scrape the rock clean of all valuable minerals, while also avoiding a collapse in the ever shifting mine's gravitational fields and temperature. Human judgment and dexterity – the feel they called it – could not be learned or mimicked inorganically.

That was why the lowest caste of society, the laborers, happily took the space mining jobs whenever they could find a worthy captain to train them up. There was a lot of money to be made in the occupation that landed on earth once or twice a year and brought back heaps of rare and valuable metals and isotopes, like gold and uranium ore and even diamonds. The savvy captains knew they controlled the supply and therefore the demand and he had a secret asteroid cache containing the rarest of metals.

As Sheetrock stood in the open roof cap, he felt cold, saltwater spray and wind grapple his body. Rain fell steadily and made the dark green Sound look misty in the runway lights. He felt more alive than he had been in nearly a year. It was a feeling space could never evoke, and it made tears swell and bubble over his vision. He loved to return home.

After a few moments, guiltiness emerged and poked at his stomach with what felt like razors. He wiped away the powdery grit of metal shavings from his scruff of a beard with the help of the rain. He was not about to delay takeoff for earth with a shower.

Recruiting miners was all too easy, earth produced thrill seekers and *entrepreneurs* at a rate of a dime a dozen. But finding talented men and women to join his drill crew that at least pretended to account for team safety up where total isolation made looking out for yourself absolute necessity was a lot harder than he would ever have imagined. That was why he often took the *cream of the crop*, as he called them at training camp, even if they were not always savvy enough to put their survival instincts ahead of their money-grabbing skills.

Sheetrock had lost his third Dynamic Positioning Operator (DPO) in nineteen months on the last run, because the idiot, a cocky twenty-four year old boxer named Jesse Jenson, could not tell when to stop a fully excavated tunnel search, even after losing sight of diamonds for over fifty feet. *What a dumbass*, he thought and sniffed back something sliding down the inside of his nostrils. The unstable mine had collapsed inward and luckily all of the other less suicidal members of Sheetrock's team had made it out in time before they were sealed beneath the avalanche.

The success rate of a space miner was roughly fifty percent, where half of the miners retire at thirty-five with enough wealth to live well or start another business even and the other half dying prematurely of any of a number of things, including respiratory illness that often stemmed from oxygen deprivation in high pressure settings (where the large asteroids contained ocean-like depths), rapid bouts of hyper-active cancer, head trauma, and of course a bevy of mining accidents. The odds were... fairly even.

* * *

Sheetrock had taken off his helmet to toast a bottle of champagne with the boys as the drill pulled out from the last haul, except it never started to pull out. Jesse took it upon herself to try and score another cache of diamond cluster and before anyone realized what was happening, the tunnel shook, and they heard a deep resonant cracking sound. Looking down they could see that metal filings had stuck to their drinks. The team looked back at the rough-hewn circular hole and the enormous whale of a drilling machine, and a dust cloud buried the silvery cylinder, filled the air, and gusted after them. They ran.

* * *

Port Jefferson was a welcome sight. The town's yachts tossed and turned in the rocky storm and the lights of Danford looked welcoming. The young captain was only twenty-nine but felt the pang of loss deeply. His friend of eleven months was dead and would never see the earth again.

Why'd you have to be such a dumb-, he sniffed loudly, *ass, Jesse?* Sheetrock thought and blew his nose on his shirtsleeve. *And it was such a nice ass.*

30

CASH MONEY

Some people have a song constantly playing in their head. Sheetrock was one of these, and he knew it. The young drill captain figured the smart people fed their soul with music every day, because one: Jesus loved music, and two: rolling down the river of audio helped keep the record from skipping. Whereas those that despised the music echoing in their brains, scoffed openly of it, and resisted it to the extreme, those people often got jarred into the realms of insanity. They beat on the player Jesus had given them and as a result their records did, on occasion, skip.

No matter the near-death run, the loss of his colleague and lover, or the freezing cold downpour, the David Byrne horns in his head blared on, and he welcomed the beauty of the earth, grimy as he was treading the soaked wooden dock. He whistled while his cargo unloaded, weighed, and purchased. It had taken all of an hour; it was the reason Sheetrock chose to land in Port Jeff in the first place: easy access to the scales and the buyers. Within another hour a quick sale had commenced.

With the payment transferred instantaneously upon completion of the cache transaction, Sheetrock walked swiftly with a slight limp toward the town's bank (his knee had blown out in a ten kilometer benefit run and the rain's moisture did it in). He had already handed each of his crew a payroll check that they knew would come into fruition once they had finished emptying the ship's cargo hold, but he wanted to confirm with his own dark eyes that his personal account totaled twenty-eight million and change. He could finally afford to spend it all.

There was a slow methodical scraping as his muddy miner's boots found the doormat outside the federal bank on the corner of Main Street. The heavy footwear was sealed, along with the black leathery jumpsuit that was made for rigorous activity in the oxygen deprived canals of space. He had not bothered changing. He was too eager.

At least the rain's washed the dust off my ass, thought Sheetrock as he walked into the bright lights of the taupe room. The large man could not have looked more out of place. A mile or two up the road was the derelict sidewalks of the Station, where none of the black market shufflers would ever have looked at his unshaven face and his stained and patched up space suit and given it a second glance. In the bank, he was almost two feet taller than the shortest tellers, and they stared open mouthed as though he was the second coming of the Messiah.

There was no one in line, but Sheetrock was a slave to ritual so he entered the velvet rope lane and followed it in three snaking switchbacks before a prim, older woman with the biggest eyeglasses he had ever seen waved him over.

"Hello. I'd like to make a withdrawal"

"Fill out the pad, sir" she said before he could complete his sentence. He reluctantly bent and wrote sloppily on the screen with a pen that was tied to the counter and did not allow his long arms to lift it far enough to be comfortable writing in the lines.

"As for the amount... Rosemary" said Sheetrock noting her nametag, "I put in for it two weeks ago, but I don't know exactly how much is in there. I want all of it."

“Very well, sir.” She tilted her round head back to look him over and confirm his face with the scan she had on the screen in front of her. It was a feat that seemed a difficult one without there being any visible sign of a neck on her, and the blue eyes behind her enormous glasses bulged in the magnification as she took all of him in.

A frantic clacking of keys was heard, as she composed herself. Rosemary, the banker, seemed to be in a perpetual hurry.

“That’s the amount you have there, sir.” She pointed down toward his screen. “The supervisor’s already verified your request and approved it. Do you have a suitcase or some kind of carrier for the withdrawal?” she asked querulously.

“Jesus please be with me today” his whisper to himself was a growl that she heard quite plainly. “I’m soaking wet and fresh off the ship. Does it look like I have a suitcase with me, Rosemary?”

“No, I don’t think so.”

“Do you have some kind of transportation case?” he asked impatiently. The round face tilted a little, like a bird’s.

“Deposit cases are available for two hundred dollars each. Are you sure you don’t want to go?”

“Listen, little lady, lord knows that twenty-eight million is not going to fit into the envelopes you normally give me my cash in, now is it?”

31

CURFEW COMES EARLY

Two large gray storage containers were brought in front of the counter, where Sheetrock paced. He signed for them hurriedly, and a resonant tone crackled and cut off the elevator music that had been playing. Everyone looked up, startled. A booming electronic voice took over the loudspeakers:

"THIS IS A CYBER ALERT: A 7 P.M. CURFEW IS NOW IN EFFECT UNTIL FURTHER NOTICE. PLEASE RETURN TO YOUR HOMES NOW." There was a short pause, and the TV announcer could be heard again in the bank.

"It appears the Cyber police" said the TV news anchor, "are hot on the trail of a fugitive known only as William Waltz, but until the manhunt is over our local Suffolk County government is forced to impose a 7:00 curfew so that residents are not harmed while this man Waltz, who is considered armed and dangerous, is brought to justice." The picture shook as the speakers boomed again.

"THIS IS A CYBER ALERT: A 7 P.M. CURFEW IS NOW IN EFFECT UNTIL FURTHER—"

"This is not good" said Sheetrock. He started to pick up the handles to the two heavy transport cases and set them down as a cough took him, long and hard. Rosemary looked at him and he saw concern in her face.

"You're bleeding, Mr. Sheetrock." She pointed her chubby fingers toward his hand. He took it from covering his mouth and saw a red streak dripping from his palm. He closed his eyes and took a deep breath trying to calm the rattle that he felt in his wincing lungs that tickled his throat and begged his body to cough without stopping. He slowed his breathing and swallowed the coughs before they emerged.

"They better not close the market."

32

CONNECTIONS

"I waited for you, my friend."

"Thank you" said Sheetrock hoarsely. He put his hands in the pockets of the leather coat he had thrown on overtop of his mining suit.

They were isolated between an open van and a line of cars. The echoes of the nearest street speaker were heard in the sloped parking lot in between the broadcasts of the clip that still blared about the curfew in the young night. The alley lot was a couple of bays over from the back of Tara's Inn and the fish market's loading dock. Murmuring could be heard amongst the raindrops, as the manhunt had caused quite a stir on the already very vibrant black market.

"The price had gone up twenty percent" said Fae Yu. She turned to the open side of the van and pushed on a round light on the ceiling. The plush inside of a two-meter long case was open, looking like a cross between a sarcophagus and a guitar case. Each side was equal in depth and shape, though one side held plush padding and a transparent breathing mask in the head section; the other side contained plastic straps, bundles of multicolored wiring harnesses, and a gleaming black exoskeleton.

"But since the morning" she said, "well, now the price is doubled... to fifty-five million, Sheetrock." Her face, normally impassive under the direst of circumstances, smiled broadly. Red flushed his cheeks.

"Jesus Christ! Where do you get off?" he asked. The rain rumbled deeply along the tin roof of the white medical van. Then all was drowned out by the sound of the curfew announcement for a minute. Impatience and fury boiled, and a large vein started to define itself on the side of Sheetrock's forehead.

"Mind your god" she said flatly when the loudspeakers went silent.

"Since this morning there has been a curfew put in effect by the government. Things will be harder to move, supply will shrink for some time" she said.

"I know all of that well, Yu. But my price has always included a twenty-five percent bonus that I'm giving to you solely for the acquiring of a new, unused prototypical unit and another twenty percent for the danger involved in acquiring such an experimental military piece of property" he growled.

"The pieces I desire would only cost me ten million dollars, used, and only twelve million clean of blood and guts and tested to function within 99% capacity. I had accounted on you adding another twenty percent on by the time I was ready to meet with you, but another 95% on top of that? You are pushing your luck."

The smuggler was a small woman, but her demeanor, her knowledge, her skills cast her in a far taller light; in the alley, her shadow did not shrink from his words but instead it grew as she stood erect.

And Sheetrock could feel the vein protruding from his head. He coughed and did his best not to double over and wince, though his body screamed for him to do so.

"Patrols continue to come down the street, causing the market to either disburse and hide temporarily or be arrested. I've waited for you for an hour beyond our newfound Cyber bedtime. This is a fully assembled unit, brand new, the first of its kind – as you know damn well. The price is what it is; fifty-five, and that is my final offer. I can get more for it in pieces tomorrow morning if I approach the right people. And I think I will."

Sheetrock grabbed the sliding door before she could slam it shut. He knew she was flustered. She had talked very fast, and in all of the years of dealings with the Cyber pirate she had never shown any fear, reluctance, or curtness, even when negotiating a tough deal. Something bothered her, but he could not afford to let it delay what he needed so badly. *I have to catch her unawares.*

With a snap of his wrist the side door of the van flew open and the thin woman seemed to reel. The unexpected move gave him the advantage, but as he pulled the scatter pistol from his coat pocket, a cold blade swung in an uppercut that smacked his wrist hard enough that he dropped the gun without a second thought.

The movement was so fluid and fast that Sheetrock had missed it when he pulled on the door and tried to get the jump on Yu. She had nearly broken his wrist with the flat part of the katana, but he knew the patience and discipline it took for her to twist the razor sharp end of the blade away from the mortal veins.

"You're lucky I like you" she said. "For a miner captain's bastard with a death wish I should have cut you into tiny pieces and sold your organs to harvesters up the road."

"That really hurts!"

She raised an eyebrow in response.

"I'm sorry" Sheetrock broke into a full minute of guttural coughing. "You know that I need that" The hacking started again and red spittle fell down his chin.

"How badly do you need this?" asked Yu earnestly. She lowered her sword and looked from the handle to his haggard face, the white in his hair, and back to the drops sliding down the steel.

He controlled the cough with deep controlled breaths. It felt like boa constrictors were clamping down on his lungs and starting to swallow them whole.

"Badly, Yu. I'm desperate... if you can't tell."

He wiped his mouth and winced as he saw the dark red that brushed off of his lower lip. *Honesty's the best policy now* thought Sheetrock.

"I inherited my old man's cancer, as well as his ship. I never should've blasted through the atmosphere this last trip. I'm all used up."

The rain patter on the roof slowed. *Thank God*, he thought. *The electrical connection will be less dangerous.*

"Why did you go?"

"Because I needed to be able to pay for the only cure, Yu."

"You should've told me" she said.

"You're a mercenary" said Sheetrock, as he bent to pick up and holster his B"9. Seeing the look of disappointment on Yu's face was more painful than the sword slap had been. "I'm sorry, I mean you've got to eat too. It's too much to ask for on credit.

"You're right about that, soldier. And you're still short I take it?"

"No way!" The two of them laughed a little.

"You can have it for thirty million and count yourself lucky that I did the dirty work on this one myself and so I'm not paying any middlemen for my troubles."

"I've got twenty-nine, Yu." She frowned. After a short swing to dry the blade, she sheathed the katana. The black and silver handle bobbed up and down in her restless hands.

"It's everything I have. I'll give you the password to my bank accounts" he said exasperatedly.

"I believe you" said Yu. "How are you going to go on living without a penny to bribe your crew into another eleven month drill campaign?"

"I sold the ship."

Now it was Yu's turn to be surprised. Her face fell. She had known Sheetrock's father, Captain Sheetrock, when she started smuggling at the age of fifteen. The S.S.S. ship was a family heirloom and all that Sheetrock's family had of value, or valued in terms of possessions on earth. *She really didn't see that coming*, he thought.

"It's how I came up with the last five million and paid off all of my debt. This machine's going to be a fresh start for me."

"But you'll be broke. What are you going to do?"

"I was kind of hoping you'd help me with that, Yu. You know you can trust me, so think about what you can get to trade once you have a militarized mech-warrior in your employ."

33

BIOHACKING

"You're lucky you don't have any of that shit in your body" said Xera. Scorn filled her words. She shook her head. Lightning lit up the empty street. They were almost to Jordan's.

"I don't go in for that kind of thing" Waltz replied. *She's regretting taking me on*, he thought. *I really hope she doesn't put a bullet in the back of my skull.* The wind scratched at his throat.

"That kind of tech" he paused and swallowed, "I've seen it ruin too many good people."

The loudspeakers boomed from the ancient trunk of a tall oak tree that was hundreds of years old and the monotonous audio became entwined in the many arms that stretched out, the long gnarled limbs reached over the entire road in their search for sun and space. There was a curfew in effect.

34

C:\>_INSTALL

The medical van's door was shut with them inside. The round dome lights were all emitting a soft glow and the steel and red colored respirators, shelves, and equipment lining the walls brought about a sterile feeling that was only mirrored in the plasticky alcohol smell in the air. Sheetrock wondered if Yu had stolen the ambulance van in case he had complications from the procedure; she had to know he was going to go through with it as soon as he got the mech-armorsuit. It was too hot to keep around without drawing pursuant thieves near.

"I thought you might be sick. Why else would you suddenly desire such a dangerous object if it had not been the only hope you had of a cure" said Fae Yu. "I consider you as close a thing as I have to a boyfriend, Ben."

"Me too" he said with a short cough. It was very hard for him to breathe, let alone talk. The gurney had been tossed, and he rested on his back strapped down to the padded bench and tried to keep completely still.

"Do you know that no one's survived this prototype's installation yet?" she asked. It became hot in the back of the small place and the slowing rain thudded ominously upon the roof whenever there was a strong blast of wind. He began to sweat in anticipation, his armpits, stomach, spine, and forehead all started to drip.

The mech-armor was groundbreaking technology that had yet to pass the experimental stages. Some twenty percent of the mech-pioneers died when having the armor installed and the other eighty percent died within the first twelve hours. The public knew nothing of this. But Sheetrock would have been dead within weeks or possibly days from the cancer anyway.

35

A:\>_SETUP

With a snap, Yu closed the metallic claw over Sheetrock's left wrist. She moved quickly then. The smooth material was made of polycarbonate ABS copolymer reinforced with carbon fiber weaves; once the nearly indestructible device was activated it would start the procedure automatically, whether the user was ready or not. There was no turning off the semi-autonomous mech system.

Sheetrock began to breathe faster and faster and labor in the task. The cancer gripped him tightly. With another clack, the bottom of the coffin case snapped into place around his ankle. And without waiting or giving warning, she twisted the case around to cover his entire back.

When the center of the hinged case made a winding sound and beeped, she knew that needles had extracted themselves from the hinges and lay along the space in his spinal column at the small of his back. As instructed, she thrust with all of her bodyweight onto the back of what surely looked like an open guitar case that was face down. And the incapacitated miner screamed like he had never done before.

All at once Sheetrock's body squirmed involuntarily and went into spasms. Excruciating and disabling feelings of absolute agony and electric numbness went back and forth in a throbbing manner. Yu sat on the case forcing it further into his spine as she waited for the mech's processor to fully load the installation program's software updates and begin to integrate with flesh and bone. Her research indicated that completely penetrating the spinal cord would stabilize him.

She admired Sheetrock. It was quite a risk he took but if it worked he would climb up in the Cyber world and make a new name for himself. First he had to beat the rabid cancer that had grown, like heavy barnacles in his chest.

As the microbots in the armor entered into his body through the needles in his spinal column, Sheetrock threw his head back and screamed. The bots came in clusters of tiny spiders that brought web strands that trailed from the mech-armor and fused with the nervous system all the way onto the targeted receptors in the brain. A smelting, a merging, went on in the body, and it was excruciating.

The unparalleled upside to the risky installation was the mech-armor's self-replicating cell regeneration technology. A host that joined with the symbiotic robotics suit found that their new exoskeleton located weak tissues and dispersed with many of its agents to remove any internal bodily pathogens or abnormalities on the cellular level; the mech forged new cells of the same type and gutted the rot. It needed a clean slate to be accepted preventing any rejection by the body. Cleaning house, by replicating each and every cell safely, purged cancers, viruses, and diseases practically upon contact. But the process was strenuous and painful as the entire body was recycled in as little as seven hours... if the body survived the process.

Yu had just gotten the leather belt and gotten it into Sheetrock's mouth when he lost consciousness. *Thank God*, she thought.

He's going to hurt plenty if he wakes up before this finishes with his cancer. She started rummaging through drawers and setting aside all of the painkillers she could find. An IV was out of the question now that the mech-armor busied itself burrowing into Sheetrock's bone and nerve structure. A large syringe was placed on the counter along with a box filled with vials of morphine.

36

ALLIANCES

The Port Jefferson train station was not far from the black market, and though the ancient train cars were rusted and had not been outright replaced or painted for a decade or two, the engineers made sure their team of mechanics kept the wheels and engines oiled and in good working order. The electric and diesel lines had both been upgraded for solar receptacles a decade earlier. Waltz and Xera Finn approached the station warily; he did not want to have another run-in with Reno until they were better prepared.

The passenger seats within were cracked and worn, but their plastic endured and served to bring many tourists from New York City to the Long Island port. The LIRR also remained one of the few available means of transportation that did not require some type of registration or tracking to come and go at will. It was a favorite of his and many of the bootleggers and black hat merchants.

“Jordan is not far” said Waltz.

“What stop?” asked Xera impatiently.

“You don’t trust me?”

“At this point, if you try to run I will shoot you down and bring in your corpse myself. All I have to say is ‘the fugitive tried to jump me’, and my life would be secure.” She replied.

“Try to keep your cool” said Waltz, and he was happy to see that this infuriated her. “We’re getting off at Huntington.”

He saw that as good as she was, he had some more experience than her, and as he treated her as a pupil and not an adversary she lost some of the 'upper hand' that she had maintained up until that point. He stretched and buttoned up his suit, despite being seated. It was important to keep in more of his body heat in the cold car. Waltz closed his eyes as though he did not have a care in the world.

Let her watch out for us, see if we're followed or marked, and worry about when our stop comes up, thought Waltz. *I have to try and work out why Cyber would wage war against me. We had one heated argument over a corrupt CEO and I'm a dead man? Could Cyber know that the deal with Wangluo was ongoing? They certainly hadn't set it up?*

Where's my handler? He's supposed to protect me. Why would he let it get to this point before I was even giving an opportunity to make good... unless he's been turned on too?

Thoughts and scenarios quickly rode through the forefront of his active mind and though he paused at each one to hear where the destination brought him, none made enough sense to get off there and run with the new place it led him. When he opened his eye a slit, Waltz could see Xera sitting erect and alert, and she was furious. He guessed that being such a higher-up in whatever society she was a cyber-warrior in she had never been treated with such impassiveness. His thoughts ran and ran.

37

MASS TRANSIT

The junkie stumbled in and out of the aisles and the train's seats. The cracked leather jacket hung loosely about a sweatshirt and flapped loudly with each new stumble. She could not see the face that was hidden within the black depths of their hood.

If Xera had been in a better mood, she would have laughed to herself about the man or woman that let their jeans hang below their ass crack in a trendy fashion that was popular while being blitzed out of their minds and clearly a victim of some chemical substance. Their flapping leather coat parodied Batman. Xera turned away to look out the window.

Waltz's reflection was there; he was an enigma to her. She regretted getting herself involved with the fugitive who had become a clusterfuck and a half. It could cost her the long 'fought' for career and even her life if she was not careful enough. His dismissive attitude and sheer arrogance, at a time where he was a known fugitive, was infuriating.

The overhead lights in the train blinked off. The rain-plastered windows went completely dark. The trails of white fog pressed closely to the bullet of a train; in the ever warming climate the weather extremes ruled, and their rain would not let up. In the dark, the junkie stumbled, rolled forward, and fell into her.

Before Xera could react, a triangular blade was pushed onto her neck. *Motherfucker*, she thought, cold and silent.

The light overhead blinked and went on. A voice rasped at Xera.

"I want everything you have... of value" the thief said. In the other hand was a shortened scatter pistol that was raised and pointed at Waltz's chest. *Who seems to be sleeping through this*, thought Xera annoyed. The barrel was cut dangerously low and could easily blow up the user as well as the target. *That would be funny*, she thought morbidly picturing the gun's bloody backfire in her mind's eye.

The hood fell back to reveal two bulbous retinal replacements. The cheaper eyes were like gray robotic goggles, without anything to hold them up. Their enormous digital pupils were divided: one remained fixed on Xera and the other on Waltz where he lie with his head back on the seat snoring softly.

"I'm going into my pocket and taking out my money" she said.

"Give it, pretty girl" the thief rasped. "I will take you too if you do not hurry up."

One large bill was raised. With a glint of the holographic ribbon across the front, it caught the thief's eye and he inhaled deeply at the sight of it.

"Put it in my pocket" said the thief.

Xera raised it slowly toward the coat pocket. She carefully parted her fingers so that there was space between the forefinger and the middle and the ring and the small fingers. Once she started in the pocket she jabbed the hidden needle into the thief's side. There was a gurgling sound and then a loud clanking as the knife and gun fell to the floor.

The cold rush filled the arms, like anesthesia. But paralysis and a pins and needles feeling, a hundred times over, ruined the thief's nervous system.

At the sounds, Waltz leaped up with a move he had prepared for the thief. But the assailant collapsed to the floor, permanently frozen.

"What the hell was that?"

"'Personal Damage. It's a personal concoction of my own. A paralyzer. He has a fifty percent chance at total recovery and a fifty percent chance at bodily paralysis for life. I think this thief and I are even."

"YOU HAVE ARRIVED AT HUNTINGTON STATION. THE NEXT STATION IS—"

Xera Finn stepped over the gap and followed closely behind William Waltz. As they descended the steel-tip steps, he quickened his pace away from the tracks and down to the crowded Huntington Station. Without giving her any sign, he pushed through a few travelers and approached a group of five beleaguered baseball fans.

He stopped by the sports group donning varying degrees of Yankee gear and looked the slightly younger and substantially bigger bodies up and down. She figured they would laugh at him. They did not.

The group reacted warily, seemed to encircle Waltz. The guy straight ahead of Waltz had a backwards Cross-Fit hat on, bulging shoulders, and no neck. And Cross-Fit-hat-guy got ideas of a reward in his mind. He had a *WANTED* printout in his hand with Waltz's mug on it.

Xera was either forgotten or completely ignored. *They probably think I'm not with him*, she thought. *I've gotten off the same train is all.* Xera went wide and strode away from them as though she did not see anything other than a crowd in her way.

No sooner had she rounded the corner of the nearest building then Waltz dove in at the Cross-Fit hat wearing behemoth. Before anyone could react, Waltz scooped up one of the trunks of his legs and threw the man with a single leg takedown. The behemoth fell flat on his back and caught a debilitating knee to the jaw before Waltz pivoted on his left foot and turned about to confront the others that converged on him.

In a blur, Waltz caught a six foot seven Jonnie Smith by his hoop earring. Waltz stabbed Smith's right eye and sent multiple jabs to the throat until his string-bean body went down. The reactions of the other three men standing there were way too slow. They all came forward at once... and stopped.

"I'm a crazy motherfucker!" said Waltz. "Don't you know that? You never mess with a crazy mother on the path!"

The three remaining persons wanted nothing as badly as they wanted to capture this Bruce Lee incarnation and release him to the local police for a hefty sum of money.

But the trio reconsidered. They looked at each other, then at the gasping figures of their friends scrambling in the puddles. There was doubt. They turned and fled.

The two downed men were abandoned as the others made for their car and in seconds drove off seeking backup lest the crazy man decide to pursue them.

38

SWIFT EXIT

Xera Finn came running up to Waltz. Her six shooter sidearm was unholstered and her immobile exterior had finally cracked with a look of utter astonishment. Of that he was happy. *At least I know she's human*, thought Waltz with an internal chuckle. He could not hide the smile with his hand fast enough.

"What the hell did you do that for? Couldn't you have said something to me?" she asked embarrassed.

"Not if I wanted to maintain the element of surprise" he said.

Anger bloomed in her cheeks. He had essentially undermined her authority. The smile dropped, became serious. He bent down to give her an explanation that was worth hearing.

Waltz grasped at something in the Cross-Fit man's pants pocket. As the hand emerged a wallet flapped open with a jingle of metal, and a long line of colors glinted below a silver badge's credentials. He pocketed the cash without giving it a second thought.

"He's a cop?" asked Xera.

Next came the string bean, Smith's pockets, and Waltz found a matching NYCPD (New York Cyber Police Department) badge. Then he held it up to the crowd that was gathering around.

"There's nothing to see here, folks. Please move on. Don't miss your trains. Police business" said Waltz. His voice boomed with authority.

After the crowd had dispersed, he whispered to Xera:

“They’re all cops alright. Hero cops. Having these humble NYCPD hero cops take me in would’ve showed off Cyber’s authority.”

“I was surprised no one was waiting for me at the Port Jefferson station, to be honest with you. But Huntington’s a main hub, and I knew this was coming—”

“You seem to know an awful lot about the train system, Waltz” said Xera. “And about Cyber’s motives.”

“You starting to think I framed myself?” he laughed.

The wallet was dropped onto the chest of the groaning man, sans cash. Rain dotted Waltz’s cash packed hand, and he wiped the back of his head with the cool water; it felt good.

They walked around the two police detectives on the ground, went to the other side of the station, and got into a muddy yellow cab. The Indian driver looked back over the pleather seat at them with a broad smile below an enormous sapphire turban.

“Where are you going, chief?” he asked. The voice was deep and harsh, the accent akin to Brooklyn without a trace of anything but native New York English.

“Storybook Height Street, please” said Waltz. The sound of approaching police sirens rent the air.

“Unit 717 heading to Storybook Height. Over.”

Waltz leaned forward.

“Hey, could you do me a favor, Mr.?” The cab driver tapped on an unopened pack of smokes and then pulled one out with his lips before turning to Waltz.

“Kleinfelder.”

"Kleinfelder?" asked Waltz in surprise.

"Yeah, my father was born pretty fuckin' far from India, in case you were wondering." Kleinfelder cackled and coughed unleashing a cloud of cigarette smoke. "What can I do for ya, pal?"

"If I threw in a hundred spot, is there any way you could get us to the other side of town in ten minutes? And here's the kicker: you can't say a word of where we went or what we looked like to any inquiring minds, Mr. Kleinfelder; do that and I'll double the hundred spot."

"Sure thing, chief! Had me at 'hundred spot'. Atta boy!" he said peeling out. "That's why I love the train route, it's discreet, it's got lots of action, it's got pretty ladies" he said with a nod to Xera, "and it pays!

Despite the incessant state of bumper to bumper traffic – a regularity of the busy north shore town of Huntington's infinite reality – Mr. Kleinfelder knew which back roads to take and which ones to avoid. The cab screeched to a stop at Patty's Corner Burger shop a block away from Jordan's house. It had taken them all of four minutes to get there, regardless of the limited visibility in the fog.

"You sure you want to stop here?" asked Kleinfelder.

"Yes."

"You don't want me to wait for you, right? 'Cause I'm not going to breathe in that crap."

"What crap is that, Mr. Kleinfelder?" Xera asked.

"Meat! The most disgusting thing on earth. Are you ready? I wanna get out of here."

A couple of big bills were handed over through the window, and then the cab was gone, lost in the nightly mist and the slow pulse of rain.

39

THE CYBER BROTHERS' HOME

It had only been a few weeks earlier that Waltz had walked up the same driveway to find his friend Doug, Jordan's brother, on the front porch doing a keg stand while a dozen partygoers cheered him on. The Port Jefferson Brewery had graciously provided their best Schooner Pale Ale for the occasion, and St. Patrick's Day was celebrated deliciously. There was an abandoned Solo cup and a few pieces of plastic bag that clung to the wet grass on the sloped lawn, remnants from the happy night that would not come again. The hedge along the borders of the porch had become overgrown and unkempt.

As they climbed the splintering wooden steps up to the old colonial home, Waltz felt sadness and weariness. The swinging bench sat at the end of the deck; it's cushions were soaked and covered in leaves, and two enormous pots that held famished crabapple trees on either side of the door. *He's certainly not been taking care of the place now that Doug's gone,* he thought.

Before Xera could attempt the top step, he held up his arm and barred her way.

"Hey, do you mind?"

"Sorry. Habit. Do you have a short range EMP with you?" he asked.

"Yes, but..."

"Deploy it now."

She looked from side to side cautiously and pulled an expensive looking calligraphy pen from out of a soft leather pouch that had been in her inner coat pocket.

There was a blink as a swift burst of light released the electromagnetic pulse, and then the two trees ejected from their pots. There was a puff of black smoke and a sound like an angry bumblebee. Each of the door wardens collapsed into wired segments made out of sharpened steel and clay tablet shards.

"Why would a Cyber Programmer arm his own house to the teeth?" she asked. "No one in the public sector knows what he really does for a living. Is he paranoid?"

"Why does gravity pull you down instead of up?"

"I don't know" she said annoyed. He put a hand on his lips pointing up at the silent sky. She lent him a pistol and he flicked the six-shooters off.

"Neither do I" he whispered.

With a crouch, Waltz prepared himself and then leaped full onto the porch. Two old planks turned up at the center of the platform and a pair of helidrones hovered out. They flew toward him immediately, but before the miniature helicopters could fire lethal tasers, he rolled to the left and avoided the bursts of electricity.

Without any pause, the two drones spread out and aimed inward so that they covered each side of the porch and could catch him no matter which way he scurried. Miniature lines of lightning snapped out from each bot. He dove and tumbled forward and onto his feet again, feeling his shirt smolder on the back of his left shoulder. *That was too damn close*, he thought. *They're going to burn my eyes out if I don't end this now.*

Instead of racing in an expected zigzag pattern, Waltz charged headlong at the helidrone hovering closer from the right side of the porch. The drone on the left shot wildly and then paused to turn one hundred and eighty degrees and save its comrade. But it was too late.

The heavy .357 Magnum's butt smashed down upon the drone on the right side and sent it to the ground where its bent propellers drove it in a circle on the wooden floor. In one motion the blow was dealt and then the gun arm lifted in an uppercut that batted the drone from the left side out onto the lawn where its loaded taser jammed and fired upon itself. There was a small burst of yellow flame and black smoke.

So you've managed to reverse engineer the force field tech that's immune to the EMP, he thought. *What else have you been up to, M.J.?*

The robotic guards were gone, taken out. Waltz looked out onto the steps and the lawn. Only the litter, the long grass, and the drone's smoking corpse met his eyes. Xera was gone.

40

DRONES

As the floorboards parted and the helidrones shot into the air, Xera backed down the stairs and hoped to God that the aged steps did not creak and draw the bots' attention.

The calligraphy pen charged for a few seconds in Xera's slender hand and then blinked. She let loose another blast of EMP. The pulse had no effect.

"What the—"

And she was cut off; a sweaty hand closed ruthlessly about her throat. The lack of air quickly forced her knees to buckle. She dropped the pen. The dim grass felt wet on her palms. The house became fuzzy and blurred unevenly with a shade of red that shrank her field of vision more and more until she remembered nothing.

41

B.O.N.E.S.

A shiny black quadruped robot pushed open the heavy front door with two horns that were sharpened to needle points. Some kind of milky poison dripped from them. The mix of the mechanical bull and Ray Bradbury's robotic dog had inspired a fast and powerful weapon called B.O.N.E.S. (for Brain Ordered National Evacuation Squad) that was semi-autonomous, requiring a human pilot to issue critical commands and perform acts of violence (so that the B.O.N.E.S. army division of bots did not turn on their masters).

B.O.N.E.S. charged at Waltz.

Oh shit.

Much of the public believed the artificially intelligent robots only worked independently to haul food and supplies into dangerous territory to bail out stranded CPU runners. The people had even voted for it. The protection of the bunkers, the majority of the human element remaining in the Cyber military, was priority, and the B.O.N.E.S. units were capable of carrying half a ton on their broad backs at a time. Since space mining had freed up rare metals and made their cost far less, the Cyber Congress passed legislation swiftly and the government mass produced tens of thousands of the two meter-long, one and a half meter-tall robots in one election year.

B.O.N.E.S. rushed at Waltz, missed him, and crashed through the porch's railing and onto the lawn. The heavy steel hoofs skidded on the slick grass and turned to face the sprawled cyber-warrior figure, the fugitive. To gain traction, B.O.N.E.S. jerked his back legs violently, kicking up turf and mud in clumps.

42

BARK LITTLE DOGGIE

Jesus, it's going to tear this whole damn place down just to spear me like a fish, Waltz thought. Is Xera dead? I have to try to get to the street and find a car. Is she dead?

The head was flat and devoid of all facial features except two deep-red eyes that glowed brightly in the stormy night.

"Come on you son of a bitch!" Waltz cried at B.O.N.E.S. *Jordan could've put any kind of poison on those fangs. Shit, here it comes.*

The freakishly quick robot approached the stair faster than he had anticipated and in one leap was up it. In a desperate effort to escape, Waltz dove straight over the top of the bot's body, even as it raised its horns in alarm. He cleared them and did a somersault forward.

The problem was that he had run out of deck. Waltz tumbled onto the splintery wooden steps and felt his collarbone crack upon impact. With a curse he struggled to turn around and back up, but as he faced the glowing monstrosity's steaming eyes, the five hundred pound beast bore down on top of his chest with its two front hooves. He screamed in agony as the bone that was surely fractured, at the least, shifted beneath the hundreds of pounds.

He was caught. The wind and rain picked up and doused his upturned face. Death would follow once the venom was applied.

When Waltz was able to stifle himself, the gyration of the beast's internal gears whined and clanked audibly up close by his ears. B.O.N.E.S. stared down and shifted its head from side to side in swift mechanical thrusts that forced another scream of anguish from the fugitive.

Waltz was pinned and his eyes scanned the bot's underbelly. Kevlar armor protected the wiring and the whirring motors, and gave the beast a hide that Waltz knew he could not penetrate with his bare hands.

Footsteps approached and he heard a faint whimper nearby. But he could not turn his head while he was held beneath the beast. The shining black head slowly pivoted inward, unnaturally, because no real bull could bend its head into its neck like that. Slowly the horns calibrated themselves back and forth until they pointed directly at his eyes.

"No" Waltz pleaded.

The bull eyes' crimson glow splashed his face, and in the cold rain he could feel their heat.

The two slightly curved steel horns inched their way down. Slowly, they continued to align with the green of his eyes. They closed in on them. A trickle of poison milk fell from each of the tips and landed on his frayed collar. He blinked and gasped; the points were about to touch him and gauge his eyeballs.

But B.O.N.E.S. whipped its mighty head to the side at the last possible moment before it was going to pierce his retinas. The experienced cyber-warrior managed to get a hold of his breathing and calm down. Despite the crushed sternum, he readied himself for an opening. *There's always a way out*, he thought.

"I know someone is watching this. I'm no good to you dead" said Waltz to the blank, red eyes. "I'm valuable. You don't even know how valuable."

The desperation in his own rasping voice disgusted him. But he wanted to live, if for no other reason than to find who was about to kill him and introduce his fist to them in person.

The gleaming horns snapped back into place and went lower down his face until they were within an inch of Waltz's eyes. He felt his ribs threatening to break under the weight of the faux animal. More white beaded at the tips and contrasted with the black surface sharply. They moved, and Waltz shut his eyes.

The bullhorns fell. Waltz gasped with terror. They moved and sliced into his cheeks just below the eyes and slid down for two inches before receding. The pain became unfathomable. His collarbone moved beneath B.O.N.E.S. and a rush of color shadowed his vision.

There was nothing but the growing fire in his face. He screamed. And in between each breath, there was the sound of maniacal laughter. Everything became like night.

43

C:\>_SYSTEM_FAILURE

“Our alliance is failed, William. You should not have come here knowing this” said Jordan.

There was no light at all... only darkness inside the basement of the house. *I must have passed out. There was a storm cellar door covered by the hedges that Jordan had emerged from*, Waltz thought. *I should have realized.*

“Where’s Xera?” he asked.

That unnerving laughter came out again, long and creepily soft, like a wheeze.

“I’m here” she said and was silenced by a kick.

“She’s tied up and waiting her turn, my friend.”

“I brought justice to those who killed your brother” said Waltz. “How can you do this?” Silence. For a moment all that he could hear was his own breathing, which was shallow with the injury to his collarbone.

“You killed her, William. And you betrayed us.”

Doug’s brother did not sound remotely like himself, yet it was Jordan’s voice.

“I did not betray Cyber. I avenged your DEAD BROTHER!” There was a kick that connected with Waltz’s midsection; the blow shook his chest and the bones there, and he screamed with anguish and frustration and pain.

“Try not to shout” said Jordan.

He laughed in a high pitched cackle that was not in any way like the one that Waltz had known back at their office.

God, what happened? thought Waltz. It was frightening.

"What happened to the young man with the bright future who was pegged to break into the cyber-warriors?" asked Waltz.

"Don't talk. It will only help the virus work faster" said Jordan matter-of-factly.

"What did you do to me?" Waltz asked.

"William, William, William..."

44

BETRAYAL

William Waltz was in pitiful shape. He was slumped over, naked, with his arms tied behind the back of the chair; his haggard face was already burning a dark red around the two thin cuts below his eyes. *My allergies are terrible*, thought Jordan, as he sneezed and shivered. He coughed and repeated what he had said. *Too damn humid.*

"William, William, William... do you know how long I studied microbiology alongside my obvious passion for computers? At first the many Bio courses helped to inspire my immersion into the code. I learned that there is nowhere on earth where a man create something that is not influenced by the powerful mathematics of nature."

Waltz's thin shoulders were muscular and they twitched with the newfound and wholly unexpected stress. Sweat beads dotted Waltz's forehead as he tried to clear his head and think of anything that would override the predicament that avenging Doug had placed him in. This pleased Jordan greatly. It was poetic justice of a kind.

"Cyber doesn't value biology. You have no way of knowing this, but we don't as a state fund anything beyond the bare minimum in the medical fields, and to make up for this Cyber buys most of its real medical tech from Wangluo – those who you deem are demons, our chief enemies – directly. They just re-label it all. The government you serve is only concerned with making cybernetics and computing transcendence, no matter the cost to its people or their soul."

"Wangluo deals with all science. They are wise and they are advanced, and they took my knowledge, my passion, and welcomed me with open arms."

"So you are a traitor" said Waltz "like Doug was."

There was a long pause. Jordan had been about to laugh when his night vision readjusted. The black basement became an indigo color and every crack and shadow was revealed to his new vision in startling detail. As he focused things became clearer, and he could make out the very pores on William's face; he could count them if he wanted to, even at ten feet away. There was only a thick blurry outline around the bodies, as though he could make out some kind of opaque aura.

Jordan walked to his adversary and with one finger wiped a line of sweat from his forehead.

Waltz did his best not to recoil audibly.

The smooth line that was now devoid of liquid; hills stood out, but Jordan could not feel the moisture on his finger at all. He played with the puddle, running it between two fingers without any other result.

"My brother was never a traitor" he said. "Only I was. He took good care of me, but then realized what was happening and he tried to stop Helena and our operation."

He recanted, but his thoughts were elsewhere, as the IV had begun to change his brain patterns. He thought happily of the coming advances. Already he had begun to tap into his entire network with his mind, as he connected by cable with an A-block's port. The prisoners could not see it, but a wire hung down from the IV in his elbow to the left pants pocket. It was how he had controlled B.O.N.E.S. and the hover drones seamlessly, without touching any physical device or enduring any delay in command.

"What did you do?" whispered Waltz.

Jordan turned and reached onto a steel shelf and pumped hand sanitation onto his palms.

"I merely infected you with a brand new retrovirus. I call it H.E.P.V. for Hyper Epo Preparation Virus. I took the formations of code and the equipped microbots and the lethal mutinous beauty and combined them all for a time bomb of a disease. It never would've have been possible to even study Ebola, as I have, if not for Wangluo."

"God damn you."

"God has little to do with this, I'm afraid" said Jordan with a chuckle that ended in a guttural cough. He leaned down closer to hear Waltz better.

"This acts as an immune system degenerate at first – for a few days – and once your body puts forward an army of white blood cells into your blood, BOOM, the Epo virus will begin to use those to breed en masse."

"Why?"

"Why, William? Well, here's the best part: I can control the artificially programmed retrovirus to proceed as slow or as quickly as I want through the electrode array linked to my arm. Cooperate with me and you can live for years without being infected."

"The field of medicine is many years away from what you're describing. Decades possibly" said Waltz.

"Nope!"

"You're insane." There was only a hoarse trail of laughter in response.

"Fine, M.J. First, leave the girl out of this. Let her go and deal with me."

"You killed Helena!" said Jordan with hate filling his voice.

45

DICHOTOMY

Carl scurried toward the cover of the two vehicles and moved his considerable bulk with an agility that Sigmund found uncanny. The rotund man was puffing, of course, and his Giants t-shirt was visibly soaked in sweat under the light of a nearby streetlamp; there was also a fresh mustard stain courtesy of a corndog from Tara's.

"You really should find clothes that fit you" said Sigmund. His dark skin was covered in patches, a young man's beard that would not come in full for many years yet, and his spidery hair was splayed out in clumps of banana curls as if to match his face.

"I had 'dis shirt since before you were born" said Carl. "It's lucky."

"I don't see how lucky it is: a new curfew, Cyber soldiers everywhere, and the freakin' rain won't stop."

As he said this, Carl tried to inconspicuously tug the white t-shirt down over the last roll of his massive gut. Then he pulled a small hilt from his belt, and in a flash of rain spatter he unfurled a butterfly knife and set the blade to Sigmund's balls.

"Woh! Come on, bud. I thought we were here to make a deal" he said and wiped rain from his eyes and held his hands up in submission.

"We are" said Carl. "But I'm tired of takin' your shit, Sigmund. Let's just see if you were planning on fucking me tonight, okay?"

God, why didn't I just get him the B8 that he wanted? thought Sigmund.

A massive paw of a hand reached up and unzipped Sigmund's tarnished coat. Carl's left palm emerged holding the B3 scatter pistol. The right hand holding the knife did not budge from the seller's junk.

"I knew it" Carl said with disdain. "You can't pull one over on me, I'm from Jersey." And he laughed raucously, as if his statement explained everything that was funny in the world at large.

Balls, thought Sigmund regretfully.

"I should put new holes in your jeans... right here." The point of the knife was pressed a little harder to the crotch.

"But lucky for you, Sigmund, you did me a favor."

"I did?" *God help me* he thought. Sweat began to pour down his temples in the pounding rain.

"Yeah, 'cause you probably know all about the B3's overheating problem and you probably know all about its scatter-mite ammo backfire. But what you don't know is that the B4, B5, B6, B7, and B8 all had their problems too, but when the manufacturer alleviated the overheating from the three they took almost half of the gun's reach, accuracy, and power away from it" Carl said.

He eyed the barrel of the B3 and cocked back the heavy chamber. Then he took the knife and in a sweep of his hand closed it and put it away.

"Hold still now" he said. "I may be a slob but I don't deserve your shit, Sigmund. Do you agree?"

He nodded in acquiescence and straightened the arms over his head. He knew he was not mentally unhinged, but he had no idea whether or not Carl was, and he had no idea what the big man in the muddy flip-flops was going to do with him.

"You see the B9 is a beautiful animal... a perfect specimen. She's efficient and does not ever jam up on you. And that's why it's so damn expensive. It's invaluable. No one can afford that."

"The B8 is close in every way except power, which was cut back to give it accuracy and to not fry your balls off with scatter mites, but that makes it a poor substitute for shootin' things in the impact aspect. Ya dig?"

"Now the B3 is practically ungettable on any black market anymore. Do you know why?"

Sigmund relaxed a little. Talk was good. Carl was still his friend. And the bootlegger would've killed him already if he had wanted to. *Or was the questioning a test?* he thought morbidly.

"Most of them three's were destroyed by law when the B8 came out" Sigmund replied truthfully, "because the newer gun reused the same outer casting as the B3 with a weaker internal spring that did not kick back with bits of bullet-mites boring into its user's skin. They didn't want to have to try and distinguish them."

"That's right" said Carl. There was a loud clunk. "Geez!"

The medical van behind them shook once and was still. Lightning flashed. Only the sound of rain and wind could be heard... then thunder boomed. Then the van rocked once more.

"I think someone's gettin' some!" laughed Carl. "Once this van's a rockin' don't come a knockin', eh big boy?"

The raucous laughter spilled from him while his protruding beer gut jiggled. Sigmund considered a frontal attack on Carl, but was unsure if he was stronger than the big man that held the gun on him firmly.

"So here's what we're going to do. You brought me a rare find, 'cause I can fix the bad blowbacks and harness the massive firepower of this bad boy. The reality is the B3 is much more valuable, with most of 'em ended up as scrap for bilges, but since you didn't know dat and you tried to fuck me... I'll pay you the price we agreed on for the B8, Sigmund. You should be happy about that. And you ought to remember that I'm your friend, so long as you don't lie to me again, 'cause I'll cut off those smelly nuts next time and feed 'em to my mutt if you lie to me again."

Carl pocketed the pistol and retrieved a wad of greasy bills that he put into Sigmund's back jeans pocket before slapping his ass.

"Now I'm gonna go finish my meal, big boy" said Carl, and he walked away into the shadows of the wet cars.

A fist of embarrassment and fury swelled up in Seamus's throat. He knew that the old bootlegger had just schooled him, and he knew that the B3 was undoubtedly worth almost as much as a brand new B9 to the right buyer. The fact that he had screwed himself by trying to deceive the balding, middle-aged slob did cross his mind.

"I got something for you, Carl" said Sigmund to himself.

He reached down and pulled a tiny handgun from his ankle. The van rocked once more and was ignored. The device in Sigmund's palm was decades old, at the least, and was not made to maim painfully with scatter bullets that sent live mites into a victim's body to debilitate them; it was made in a day where a gun had one purpose: to kill.

The piece was cocked back with a click and then a wrenching and tearing of metal sounded. He turned his head. With a crash the medical van's sidewall burst open and a heavy mechanized shadow emerged and in a leap landed full on Sigmund's back severing his spine and neck. Pieces of metal shelving and shining chrome tools glinted on the pavement around him and sparkled brightly just before all swiftly went dark.

Carl did not so much as turn around at the noise. He was already onto his third corndog.

46

CONSCIOUSNESS

The stench filled Xera's nostrils and turned her stomach. As she woke fully, she found her head was heavy and her body was a lot less responsive than it should have been. *What the hell happened?* She thought.

The smell charged to her memory forefront and helped cognition. *Chloroform*, she thought. *He must have snuck up on me and used chloroform. Shit.* The old ways sometimes proved very effective and simple. A chemical soaked rag had taken down the careful, meticulous, and dangerously talented spy in seconds. What alarmed her further was the thought that anyone who had chloroform handy must have been experienced in kidnapping.

It was utterly dark, and Xera could not see anything. The burning in her wrists meant that bonds had been tightly closed about her. Moving sent sharp pangs through her legs, spine, and shoulders as well. Her hearing was muddied, as though everything had to pass through deep water before it reached her ears. Echoes of someone yelling turned her from pain to curiosity.

William Waltz, the fugitive, that was her newest client, and he was in deep. She remembered. His friend Jordan on the inside turned out to be... a betrayer. Everything turned out to be wrong on the inside. A folding chair cut into the upper part of her back and she squirmed in it. Her head hurt, and she drifted, dozed, and remembered. All went black as she grasped onto the slippery thoughts.

47

VENDETTA

"You killed Helena!" cried Jordan.

The rain's heavy fall and the night's descending temperatures produced a spray of thick, grayish-purple mist that poured in the unseen windows and filled the basement, as though it were reflecting Jordan's very mood. Waltz's body lurched against the bonds and the chair shuffled forward.

"Hold still" said M.J. quietly. His composure regained, the control struck more fear into the un-expectant victim than any amount of yelling could hope to accomplish in a week's time. "Hold the fuck still."

Waltz shook once more, his body involuntarily betraying him, and then was still as Jordan drew closer. His semi bionic left arm reached up and traced the cyber-warrior's head before grasping a hold of the temple with splayed fingers. A jolt went through from spine to brain and jarred Jordan. A rotten taste, like months old tomatoes, filled his mouth and swelled in his throat, stuck.

He reeled and stepped back. The entire cloudy room had brightened drastically and his palm itched where Waltz's short hair had connected with his tingling skin.

"Careful now, M.J." he said to himself. "We got a fighter o' fires here. And he's all juiced up, ready to try and battle, but he doesn't know the virus is on the inside right now charging on to the brain stem and on down to the tailbone and the toes" said Jordan. "You can't out-grind a grinder!"

Then he barked. An incoherent string of sounds emerged and were loud and guttural. He shouted gibberish until the sound of rain pelting the tiny basement windows started to play on his nerves, and he stared upward and was silent.

"You have no idea what I can do, William. It's the power to control... and to tap into the ether of the whole of cyberspace. I can feel the body's cells. I mean, I'm only just starting to grasp the possibilities myself."

A sound of spinning props hummed and a helidrone flashed a red sight-beam onto Waltz and then fired a short, but concentrated blast of electricity. He yelled and thrashed and Jordan rushed up to him and grasped both of his hands around the trembling temples.

There was a beep, and a monitor and an open laptop turned on simultaneously with a flicker of blinding light in that dark place. Jordan flexed his left hand and bicep; he folded and unfolded his fingers slowly. The manipulation of his extremities now controlled a fully functional operating system live. But it was more than that. He was inside them. And they were grinding inside him.

48

MISSING HACKTIVIST HQ

Thoughts drifted far away from the precarious situation to William Waltz's home. He knew he could never go back there. The likelihood was that the entire place and all its secrets – including the rumrunner tunnels – would be utterly pilfered. In the dark canvas inside of his eyelids, a vision of the weapon burned bright as he imagined using it to carve his way to safety.

Regardless of the futility in this line of thought, Waltz knew that in order to make something of the situation he was in, where he was tied to a chair by an unhinged genius, he had to disconnect his mind from the present. He had to forget the basement's smell of sweat, the dank air, and the chemicals and find a solution. But he could not come up with anything. The madman raved inaudible grunts and screams that could not have resembled language, and concentration was elusive.

Waltz replayed the last hours he had spent in his place before Cyber authorities had narrowly missed assassinating him. He tried to ignore the fact that if he had just taken the time to unlock the exo-gear when the assault began he would not feel naked and soft and responsible for the mercenary cyber-warrior that was trying to bail him out and was tortured in the process for her troubles. The exo-gear was housed in a massive hundred year-old safe that he had painstakingly inserted into the cement foundation.

In the basement he had found the treasure cove when he moved in; the safe was left unnoticed by the previous owners and had not been opened. After he had picked the combination with a stethoscope, he carefully removed the vacant box and lined the hole in the foundation with x-ray proof lead. Then he dropped the five hundred pound safe back into its hole and carefully crafted a cement door over it – with lead on the inside – that seemed by the casual viewer to resemble normal cracks in a typical cement basement floor; he had carefully made more cracks in the surrounding area to add to the illusion and when he was done the safe's door was easily accessible with a thin metal rod, but the opening to the cement trapdoor was indiscernible to anyone looking at the floor.

After the gunshots, Waltz had rushed through the secret passage and descended to the basement and then on to the first of the rumrunner tunnels. He had rushed right past the safe, where he could easily have stopped and in ten to twenty seconds gotten his exo-gear .

He thought back further. A dive for his desk would at least have yielded his smartphone to him from amongst the stacks of books, vintage tin robots, and his ornate hourglass. Though Waltz relied on computational technology to perform the majority of his day's activities, he also knew the importance of unplugging for periods of time in order to not only retain but to relish in his humanity as a living, breathing being.

Along that line of thinking, Waltz had picked up a few hobbies over his thirty years: he played the guitar skillfully; he read a great deal of books (via paper, never electronically because the idea of words being beamed at him felt like radiation and freaked him out to no end); and he liked to collect things, particularly old things, because history interested him. He loved their style as no one had for a long time.

It was part of why he had moved to one of the oldest town harbors smack in the unofficial middle of the island. Port Jefferson was an old trading post and famous for its involvement in the 1930's Prohibition period. Bootleggers meshed with the constant influx of sailors, fishermen, and travelers that preferred the rural woods and farms of eastern Long Island over crowded homes in Manhattan and Boston. It was an old fashioned kind of place.

Among the aged homes, wooded lanes, and quaint business cabins that sporadically dotted the countryside were plenty of eccentric nooks and hidden corners that Waltz used to double-back and lose pursuers. There was no shortage of hills and he had learned the many paths that trod between them.

There he had once encountered a diseased mountain lion in the dead of night. It had escaped from an underfunded ecology site in Holtsville, because such animals were not typically found on Long Island (being bereft of mountains). It had made the mistake of having eaten a rabid dog.

A road was nestled away, a mile or so from civilization, and the hungry cat attacked Waltz without warning. The dry summer dust rose in the air, like smoke, and choked his throat as he skidded in the dirt with the mountain lion on top of his back. The backpack he wore had saved his spine and organs from being torn into pieces by the clutching claws. His life was one big reaction, it seemed, so with a turn he tumbled over and in his mind lined up the red cross of the cyber sight and targeted the top of the cat's skull, dead center.

The heavy carbon fiber exo-gear resembled dark, metallic bones that rested on the forearms and then became skeletal, as a statue hand that was molded to his palm. The exo-gear gave him lethal knuckles with increased damage infliction and precise control over how much force was used, and with. With a single swing downward, there was a thwack and the mountain lion fell unconscious to the forest floor before it could infect him with rabies.

The refrigerator held a hidden compartment within its door. The blood stained, scraped, and trusty spare exo-gear shirt might still be hanging up. Or it might very well have been found and destroyed, along with his entire house. If he could just plug in through the exo-gear , escape would be all too easy. But he could never go back there again. He had lost his home.

A sudden influx of rancid smell raked at his senses and knocked him out. Xera screamed his name. He jerked wide awake to the here and now of the basement torture chamber in Huntington.

49

FOG

The foggy basement shimmered violet, as Jordan turned his attention to his restrained captives. Both of them threw themselves forward in an attempt to break free from the chairs they were tied to. He heard Waltz curse softly.

"You're finally scared of me" said Jordan.

He approached them with an exposed piece of wire. It was stripped and the razor sharp strands of copper were splayed out. He flicked at the wire between his fingers as though he were tossing a coin up in the air.

Across the multitudes of striated solenoids, electricity leapt on feverishly. The normal state of humanity did not allow for the conscious recognition of such affairs. But Jordan knew that he had evolved past humanity. He was becoming the cyborg he had always dreamed of.

Jordan looked within and saw, starting at the exposed IV in the crook of his arm, the pinging balls of light that rode the train tracks faster than was discernable; he saw dancing fireworks racing through his synapses and out of his fingertips. He saw part of his own soul's essence enter the air around him – electricity – and seek out the wireless antenna where his commands could link directly to the digital databases.

Jordan's thumb made a soft flick on the wire. He stepped closer to them. A string of curses and grunts of physical distress fell on his ears, as they slammed their bodies against the chairs that held them tightly.

"I wouldn't exert yourself, William. Your immune system's taking quite a hit."

"Fuck you."

There was a scrape, a flick of Jordan's thumb on the wire's bristles. Another set of computers lit up and their monitors were in screen saver modes showcasing the message: *DAMN YOU TO HELL, WILLIAM. You killed her.*

"Do you see the kind of power I'm wielding?" asked Jordan. Gesturing around to the humming computer cubes that he had turned on through the wireless energy that he had tapped into with his receptacle.

He knew he looked crazy. "What you must think of me now? I'm becoming a God" he finished with a single, shrill laugh.

"We don't have to believe in Gods to know that demons are real" said Waltz.

The smile slipped from Jordan's flushed cheeks for all of a few seconds. He flicked the cord's end. *Flick. Flick.* The grin returned with a vengeance.

"Don't go anywhere, folks. This one's coming directly... to your fingernails!" There was a pause as both Waltz and Xera held their breath.

"Ladies first!"

Xera shrieked hysterically. Jordan pushed up to her face and kissed it. Then he backslapped her. Her head whipped back and stunned her long enough for him to get a good grip on her left wrist. A jarring pain cut through him but was ignored. He flexed and bent back her wrist to the point where it was about to break.

Then he raised the wire up in front of her wide eyes. Piles of little pasta elbows seemed to fall from his arm. He shook them loose and flicked at the wire, once, twice, three times. *Flick. Flick. Flick.* She bucked, but her wrist was slowly raised up over her head all the same.

"Leave her alone!" yelled Waltz. Xera screamed.

In one smooth motion, like threading a needle, the bare wire was thrust under her fingernail. She cried out louder and louder, and then the delicate tissue underneath gave way as Jordan buried the ends deep within. The nail started to lift off of her thumb to make way for the wire being forced into her finger, and Xera passed out.

There was a distant hum of large computer fans starting up and the click of electronic lights in stacks of cubed towers on a far shelving unit. The entire length of the crawl space behind Waltz began to light up their many bulbs and made the dark room echo the jungle where the insect eyes alone emitted light in the dead of night. Jordan felt the hazy plexiglass emit soft purple shadows through the vented pinholes as the particles passed from his body to the machines and back to the air as heat. The computers seemed to grow more excited as Jordan did.

"Thank God" said Waltz seeing Xera's head slump when she went unconscious.

"Oh, but we're not done" said Jordan creepily. "There's still another end to the line after all."

And with that Jordan took the wire loosely in his hand and began to trace it back from her thumbnail and up over his shoulder. The other end of the piece was also exposed. He grasped through the ten feet of the cord, found the end, and licked it. Then, with a wink at the cyber-warrior, he stepped over to the nearest power strip.

"NO!" screamed Waltz. But the bare wire went deftly into the hole and a sound of zapping filled the basement. The smell of burnt meat took hold as Xera jerked and burned and the socket smoked.

On a formica countertop to Jordan's left there were twelve ancient computer monitors that were lined up and plugged in. In a fit of conceit, he turned on all of them, one by one, with his mind. Some of the monitors had huge backs that dwarfed their square screen sizes even, and on each of them was a portion of a microscopic view. Cells swam and were swallowed up by other strange looking cells that seemed to have runes built into their jelly-like amoeba body. He had views of microscopes' vision that traveled across twelve separate screens.

"It's the virus! And I control it all from here." He tapped at the protruding IV in the crook of his elbow. The ache there reverberated throughout his body. But it felt good. "I'm waiting for your eyeballs to start bleeding, chief."

Jordan seized Waltz by the temples. His hands shook blurrily. The air seemed to be full of maggots.

50

NICK'S GIRLFRIEND

Nick Reno scratched at the pencil-thin mustache he was starting to grow and uttered a grunt. The heart that the young woman and lanky dude had sold him was sabotaged. He did not know why most people grew mustaches, but personally he enjoyed playing with his facial hair whenever possible. He tugged on the short fibers and frowned. He had been screwed and was about to take out his frustration on the poor family that sat gagged in front of him.

"They screwed me." He would not have thought it was possible a day ago after the move to secure the bar embedded him in Tara's. He did not think anyone who knew who he was would dare to risk royally screwing him.

"Maybe they didn't know who I was... shit... I must be going soft in the balls" he said.

Shelly Nadramowitz, his soon-to-be ex-girlfriend and the mother of a seven year old daughter, pulled on his pant leg with hands that were tied together by duct tape. Tears streamed down her face. The bandana was tied tightly and separated her head in two, like a puppet.

"Bring me that pipe" said Reno.

Vincenzo, a man who was as wide as he was tall, waddled over with a smoking bong and proceeded to cough for a full minute from the effort. Reno bent his head to the glass tube; he needed to think through things clearly.

"Hey kid, you want some next?" asked Vincenzo with a laugh. Shelly's daughter shrieked and stifled it immediately. She wore a Betty Boop t-shirt that was long enough to be a nightgown and was standing up against a wall with her back facing the rest of them in the rundown crack house.

Exhalation. The smell of something sweet followed the plume of smoke into the room. A rush of newfound energy and a glorious dose of bliss flooded Reno's cells. He closed his eyes and spinning circles of color whistled by, like streamers and Chinese dragon floats hovering over a parade.

When the organ transplant had been removed and turned over for a full scan, he had come upon the eyeliner pencil sticking a few inches out of the precious heart's right ventricle. The stick had been stabbed in as far as it would go. The heart could not be decontaminated after that and therefore, could not be used. It was sabotage, and that was just mean.

The bong was packed with a less-than-lethal combination of pot, crystal shards, and opium and bubbled harmoniously as his less than faithful life partner held desperately onto the leg of his jeans and silently begged his forgiveness. The bowl lifted and the line of white smoke billowed up into his mouth.

It was possible that the bikers that had sold the heart to the lanky man in Tara's Inn had been the ones to ruin it, but not likely. For one thing, even though he would be the first to admit that he was no judge, he could not see either of those particular bikers in that shade of mascara.

The young girl wailed suddenly. Reno kneed Shelly away from him and pointed at her daughter with his filthy, long pinky nail.

"Shut the bitch up! Calm her down now, Shelly. She's your blood."

There was the sound of heavy steps as Vincenzo rushed over and raised the bandana up to the little girl's mouth. "How did that gag come undone, Vincenzo?"

"Her head's too damn small."

"Then crush it like a grape!" said Reno. "Shelly, if you don't keep her quiet I'm going to cut her tongue out."

Horror rounded Shelly's eyes as she raised her taped arms up to console the child. Despite the replaced bandana, the daughter's hysterics became more audible as she realized that the bad men would really hurt her.

"I need to think." He breathed deeply from the tube and exhaled a long, thin line of smoke smelling of roasted fruits mixed with something tart.

If it was not the bikers, then that left the pair that actually sold the defunct heart to him. They had saved his ass as the owner of Tara's returned unexpectantly to unload rounds after him, which earned them more credibility than taking the organ off of the bikers ever could; bikers looked mean, but most did not have it in them to not be sweethearts from day to day.

But Reno was not sure why the two would save his life and turn around and bend him over to screw him. It was an embarrassing and frustrating dilemma that enraged his sharpened senses. Unlike most of the addicts he dealt with in his day job, he did not succumb to a dulling of the senses, or a lessening of his wits. He did party with the best of them, however. And when he was frustrated and embarrassed, he could not keep the rage inside. His body would not allow it.

Shelly's daughter calmed down enough to stop making noise. Reno did not know her name, but was glad. He wanted Shelly's torment to be slow. If he killed the little girl outright then the woman's worst suffering would be far too quick and she would happily accept death afterward. It was not the way he wanted it to go down. Breaking people was an art that took time and the release of his own anger, in small, measured bursts of pain.

51

NIRVANA

Jordan felt happier than he had ever known was possible. His head felt clearer. And in the orgasmic state of nirvana, he let go of Waltz's temples and stepped back, tripping over a bundle of wire as he did so. When the floor grabbed hold, Jordan bit his tongue in surprise. Sharp pain and a tide of saliva that was all too bitter, metallic, and coppery filled his mouth.

52

THE SICKNESS

William Waltz squinted his eyes as close to shut as he possibly could while watching the sick, shaking man grasp his temples. The smell of decayed flesh was almost as unbearable as the worms that fell onto his head and neck in wriggling clusters from Jordan's left arm. The crawling proceeded down his cheeks.

Waltz clenched down. He was lethargic and weak from the drug but waited with his muscles taut for an opportunity to catch his kidnapper unawares all the same. Xera sat beside him, panting, as she tried to ignore the wire that had been thrust beneath her thumbnail. She refused to lose consciousness for the same reason that Waltz stayed alert: she was a warrior that waited for an opening and would not give up until Death approached.

With each quiver of Jordan's left elbow more of the hatched larvae surfaced and dropped. More of the maggots landed on the top of Waltz's head, while others that had previously fallen climbed up his exposed neck at an agonizingly slow pace. The urge to scream and the need to lose it approached the point of involuntary action.

Jordan must have been sick for weeks. The government sanctioned biotechnology for its employees who not only had clearance to wield them but also understood and agreed to take the risks, so long as they appeared before their doctors every other week for testing. They did this to deter biohacking. But every piece of biotech Cyber issued had traceable beacons built into their casings, and even a genius like Jordan must not have had a way to fool those securities.

He had gone for the street where worms contaminated most of the black market Receptacle IV's. And he had obviously not sought the opinion of any doctor, even after he had already administered the biotech, despite the risks. He had to have known them. To grind one into his own body would be mad. There were no safety guarantees behind the fish market. Jordan's seller might have claimed that he had acquired a stolen government-issued unit, but the likelihood that one was smuggled out of Cyber, unused and entirely devoid of parasites was almost impossible.

What began as an atypical infection, as was not out of the normal for a spider IV, grew. The flesh had succumbed and the infection spread fiercely. And Jordan was too lost being 'plugged in' to notice, not that it would have mattered. He did not see or feel the parasites feed and grow exponentially; they emitted a flesh-eating secretion – similar to the brown recluse spider's – that deadened tissue at an alarming rate. The gangrenous sections became food and housing for the microscopic tadpole spawn to eat, grow, and transform into acidic bio-worms.

Jordan clamped onto his temples hard. Waltz expected his skull to cave in from the pressure. His neck strained under the weight of the defector. Then, for no discernable reason, the grip was gone.

Jordan stepped back as though stung. A wide grin announced itself loudly and then slipped as quickly as it had arrived. Whatever funny thoughts Jordan had were interrupted as he teetered and tripped over a thicket of power lines and fell to the floor. A gasp escaped as he bit his tongue painfully.

Sensing the time slow to a final opportunity, Waltz's opportunity, he leaped up with such force that he broke the back of the wooden chair. He immediately fell to the ground, hard, face forward. But one duct-taped wrist came free of the flimsy wooden arm, and that was all he needed. Waltz was able to stretch his free hand to his ankle and pull a pocketknife from his sock.

By the time Jordan had untangled his feet, Waltz sat up and without the slightest hesitation threw the small blade into his captor's eyeball. Hands flew up in the air in response and then fell still with the rest of the crumpled corpse. Blood and white gelatin oozed from the socket around the hilt and a thrashing of tremors took hold of the body. It went quiet for thirty seconds and then started again.

Waltz sat drawing deep breaths. It was only when the monitors began to blink off, row by row, and slowly fade the room to black, that he knew Jordan was dead. The fugitive crawled forward, dragging the base of the chair with his legs, and retrieved his knife. He touched the two parallel cuts that ran down his face.

"Do you think he really put anything in the robot's fangs?"

"He was pretty much out of his head, totally cuckoo, for quite a while there. My guess would be no" she said. "It was probably just leaking oil."

"You're free" whispered Xera.

"In some twisted sense of irony, I guess you could say I'm free again... for now" Waltz replied. He sliced open the taped bonds and threw the chair's remains at the Formica table; computers toppled over, like dominoes. "I wish I was really free though" he said with a brief smile.

"You are not there yet" Xera said answering his rhetorical question obstinately. "But you will be when we get you fixed up." He freed her, and the two stretched the cramped muscles in their arms and legs and rubbed them back and forth. She held out her mangled hand and the bloody thumbnail was already starting to look like it would fall off.

"Are you okay?"

"I will be once I find some peroxide or something."

"Even Jordan must've had some antibiotic cream or a first aid kit in the house somewhere."

"So" she said.

"So?"

"So where do we go from here?" she asked.

Where indeed? he thought.

53

FORWARD

Fae Yu found her friend and one-time lover collapsed face down in the middle of a dead-end road. He groaned as she turned him over but would not wake. She wiped the muddy puddle water from his face and winced as Sheetrock wheezed audibly and coughed up a charred ball of bronchial tissue and clotted blood.

Luckily the neighborhood had yet to notice the unconscious bulk in the dim light of the block's single street lamp. Though his mech-armor made him look more like a buffed bodybuilder in a wetsuit than Iron Man, if anyone saw such an out of the ordinary person passed out in the road they were likely to report it to the authorities post-haste.

54

A MIRACLE OF MODERNITY

His body convulsed harshly again. Bits of green, red, and brown globs ejected from his lips. This went on for ten terrible minutes. Then he stopped breathing.

She squeezed his enormous cheeks and shook his head to no avail. Yu gathered herself; she was prepared for this. Without pausing as much as three seconds to think, she unsheathed the wrapper from the adrenaline syringe with her teeth and punctured Sheetrock's armor, his breastplate, and the wall of his heart. There was no response.

It was puzzling. She had followed the mech-armor schematics to the letter and hit him right within the maroon circle that was put there to show medical professionals where the armor's one weak spot was made thin in order to allow needles through.

"Come on, Sheetrock. I can't carry you."

A thought found its way to the front of her mind: *the solution is almost always sitting there, right in front of your face, taunting you.* And in a rare "ask and you shall receive" moment, which she found most delightful, a solution presented itself. The syringe's plunger had not been pushed down.

"If you were awake, you'd be laughing your ass off at me" said Yu. She sent the adrenaline home and stepped back. Sheetrock instantaneously sat bolt upright and rolled over and leaped to his feet. He ran toward the woody lane at the end of the road and stopped after a few seconds, bewildered.

He turned back to her and was happy to see a familiar face.

"Thank the Gods you're alright."

"What the hell just happened?" rasped Sheetrock. "My chest burns." She could see his breath. The cold rain beaded on Yu's face, but she could tell from the steam rising from the top of his head that he did not feel the temperature at all.

"You underwent minor surgery, my friend. An occasional heart stoppage is a small price to pay"

"What?" Sheetrock bellowed with incredulity.

"A small price to pay for" Yu finished her sentence, "when you make use of an instant cure for cancer."

"Jesus, you're right."

"Count your blessings. You survived it, old man."

"I can breathe easy again" said Sheetrock in surprise and awe. He stretched and heaved in with all of his might, and his diaphragm contracted and his chest filled with air. His lungs swelled and pressed on the inside of his chest cavity, which was not unpleasant. "That feels better" he said.

"I think it was worth it too. All of those long hours away from earth, all of the busted relationships that sent the ladies and gents screaming into the night, all of the poor members of the crew that never made it back home off of some random, freezing rock floating in some far asscrack of space, and my father's ship, my family heirloom and the livelihood of generations: all were sacrificed for this one chance, not just to survive, but so I could live a better life and if – God, help us – I have kids then they can get a much better shot at striking it big without slaving in a self-made mine and waiting for the ash of it to cut you down in your prime" he ended harshly.

He stood erect and put his arms over his head. He saw the patch of lung and blood and cancer behind her and made a dark jelly of it beneath his mechanized boot. Yu held her arm out and Sheetrock took it, and together they walked down the lane back toward the parking lot where he had utterly destroyed the medical van's wall.

"Don't expect to get any of those damn kids out of me, honey" she said with a squeeze to his bicep. He started to laugh and wheezed and coughed in pain; but a smile followed soon after he got himself under control.

"Hey forget about it, babe" he enjoyed adding the pet nicknames even though he did not know what it really meant for them. "Now there's plenty of time to change your mind."

"I think you should focus on putting some money back in that empty bank account of yours first" said Yu with a laugh. The rain continued to douse them, but she was the only one of the two of them to actually feel it; body heat was conserved and kept at an optimal state, including temperature, within the mech-armor, which also happened to be waterproof.

"I just hope we can get Cyber to talk to me. I don't want to try and cross the Atlantic in this thing but I will if it's the only way I can get by."

"What do you mean 'we,' Sheetrock?"

"There's no way I could negotiate a gun-for-hire contract with the big boys on my own. They're liable to take my suit and my spine with it even if they have to rip it straight from my back. I need your negotiating skills to prove my worth to them for all of the off-the-books work they might have."

"And you still want to be an undercover man?" said Yu.

"You better believe it, babe. Have you seen their pension plan?" asked Sheetrock. "I might be rich in no time, but I want to retire in ten."

"I'm wondering, 'will we get to see their pension plan too?' Is that what you mean?"

She toyed with him. The partnership they held was largely business and perfunctory convenience, the friendly and the sexual business, but there was no denying that they cared for one another.

"You drive a hard bargain" he said coolly.

"Ouch, I think that offer's just been revoked, Sheetrock. Best of luck with your next one."

He took her in his arms then and kissed her strongly.

"That's a start" she said.

Sheetrock kissed her stronger still. They had reached the torn open van and maybe it was the curfew in effect, or the incessant rain, but no one had looted its medical equipment yet. The lot was deserted. And neither of them cared in the least.

55

STORM'S COMING

Xera and Waltz emerged from a patch of bushes and ran to an overhang to escape getting drenched. The town's old-fashioned clock tower struck six o'clock. It was a cast iron cube with four timepieces (one facing every direction) perched atop a streetlamp pole. The curfew was temporarily lifted with the sunrise and would return that evening. In the meantime, they were free to seek an inconspicuous way out of Huntington.

"Shouldn't we look for the closest bus stop?"

"No, we're going to visit a friend of mine" said Xera. "But first I'm going to try and get us a car."

He raised his eyebrows to protest, but she shut him down with a finger to the lips. She instructed him to stay put and, without waiting to explain, dashed off down the sidewalk.

The rain seemed to part to welcome her in and then swallowed her whole. William Waltz wondered if he would ever see her again. He knew he was not worth the trouble he was putting her through. But ten minutes later a shining red Mini Cooper Volzilla pulled up to the curb in front of him.

Xera stepped out of the hydro sports car, waved him over, and climbed back into the rental car quickly to lower the rain's volume to a whisper. The local Hertz owner had been very accommodating to her; she, being a regular customer with a bright smile and an invigorating shape, had no trouble in procuring a cash arrangement that would keep their doings off the books, while mobilizing them in style. The car had satellite tracking, of course, but all that meant was that Hertz had an alias as a name for the renter and a location that a standard magnetic jammer would skew a couple dozen miles from the reality of the situation.

Waltz climbed in beside her and flicked the moisture from his sponge-like hair.

"We're going west" she said.

"Why?" asked Waltz impatiently.

"His name's Joshua Franciscus."

"Franciscan, who? Why?" he asked dejectedly.

With Jordan's betrayal and madness, this little bit of added mystery from Xera Finn was too much to bear; Waltz became unnerved and furious, as anxiety set lockjaw in him. *Jesus*, he thought. *My one friend in the world was not only murdered two weeks earlier but had been forced to turn and work for his sworn enemy* (though being around Xera, who his gut told him was a 'straight shooter' made him rethink whether or not Wangluo and all of the other outside cyber governments weren't as evil as they were made out to be).

"He's a true artist. He can manipulate the human being, like you've never seen" she said with admiration teeming in her voice.

Waltz struggled to relinquish the meeting of his grinding teeth. A growl escaped but his mouth would not move right away. When he had unlocked his tongue, Waltz asked: "Could you be any more vague?"

"Yes. I could."

An uncomfortable silence filled the inches between their seats as the street unrolled before them. Xera let the autopilot take them where they were headed; the steering wheel before her seemed to move of its own accord while she raked her eyes and massaged the webbing between her thumb and forefingers, seemingly ignoring him. She was very careful to avoid touching her injured thumb.

Waltz knew she was hiding something important about this 'friend' of hers. *At least she has friends that are above the ground*, he thought. *How bad could it be?*

"What did you mean when you said, 'he can manipulate the human being, like you've never seen?'" he asked.

"I just hope he'll see us like this" said Xera brushing away his query as quickly as it came to him.

"Like what?"

"Without an appointment."

"You have got to be kidding."

"'Fraid not. He's a stickler for... um... his rules... for his own little world. You see he's the sun, and we're going to be lucky if we can become the planets orbiting around him. It's an ego thing."

"I'll talk to him" he said.

"There's no talking to him. That'll only make it worse. He'll turn whatever conversation you lay at his feet around in circles upon circles and wear you down with his rambles of half-truths mixed in with outright lies. Nothing you can say will make him feel anything toward anyone. He has no sympathy and less than no empathy. It's amazing that he's as flamboyant as he is, but maybe that's only camouflage. What I can tell you for sure is that he's a sociopath that flirts with being an outright psychopath. And he's ruthless."

"How the hell are we supposed to get him to work with us then?" asked Waltz frustrated.

"We'll have to give him something he wants. There's no other way" she said matter-of-factly.

"What does he want?"

"Who knows? We'll find out when we get there, I'm sure. I just hope what he wants is more valuable than the bounty on your ass, William. Don't worry too much. We're on friendly terms, he and I. And I'm sure he'll want something worth a lot more than that Cyber reward."

"Great" *I am so out of my element. Why didn't I go with my escape plan for leaving this freaking country? Vindication? They're going to kill my ass,* he thought.

"If it's any consolation, he has no love for authority, despises it, in fact. Your story might – no he won't give two shits about your story. But he does like people owing him favors, that's for sure."

As she finished talking, a patch of sky brightened ahead. It did not reveal any blue, but the black clouds seemed to give way to a dense mass of light gray cloud hung off of the horizon as though it were too heavy to stay upright for long. Without warning a bright stalk of lightning slammed into the field near the road and rippled with blinding tendrils for a long second. Thunder followed and shook them in their seats, and another vine of electricity whipped down in a shot.

"Holy shit!" Waltz said as his frightened body jumped up against the seatbelt involuntarily.

"Goody! I love storms!" cried Xera. The wrinkles were there, just touching the outside of her eyes, but with her smile she looked so young. "Oh, geez. I can't believe I just said that out loud." With a steady palm, she gently pushed him back into his seat by the shoulder. "Relax and try and enjoy it. It's beautiful."

Her voice had transformed; the attractive and mature twenty or thirty-something year-old businesswoman and spy became a curious and intelligent eight-year old girl that was more in touch with the world than Waltz could ever claim to have been just then. She loved driving into the middle of freak storms, even when there was a chance of having her eyebrows burnt off. And he loved this appreciation of the wild lightning almost as much as he appreciated her voluntary oneness with something so far removed from the artificial planetary grind that it was devoid of technology and natural, like people used to be. It calmed him. Both looked out of the glass ahead and drank in the serenity, and each had dangerous, thunderous smiles.

56

CYBER HQ, NYC

"Wait for me in the car if you don't want to get your ass handed to you."

"I want to go in" said Sheetrock wistfully.

"After I get them to sign the Order of Preservation prelim, you can go in. Not before. They'll probably want a demonstration before they sign a contract anyway – I know I would – but you can't go up until they're ready and committed to hiring you."

A look of annoyance passed between them.

"I will kick your ass if you keep that up, hun. And no amount of armor will make the slightest difference."

With the rickety remains of the van, Fae Yu and Sheetrock crossed the crowded Brooklyn Bridge where protesters marched on the sidewalks. He realized that she rarely said so much at any one time and shrugged. They made their way into the Lower East Side.

An enormous black and blue glass skyscraper leaned over the dwarfed buildings in the area. The former hotel was a geometric eccentricity. The building had once kept high-end clientele happy by providing them some of the city's best views from its top floors. That was before Cyber had seized the skyscraper to use as their New York City headquarters.

As they drove closer to Cyber, the strangely angled walls that stuck out from the main section of building reached out toward them. The towering shadow was intimidating. Sheetrock knew that within each one of the checkered windows dwelt an incessant surveillance force probing everything within the bounds of the city and the continent and all of Cyber. And this Cyber headquarters was where they were headed in search of work.

Yu could not have been more self-conscious of the missing side door on the medical van as they pulled up on 107 Rivington St. and started down into Cyber's underground parking lot, audibly rattling, like a bucket of bolts being carried. He could see her twitch as every bump caused the equipment in the back to shift. The small ambulance did look like it had run over a roadside bomb. *Wait 'til they get a whiff of me*, thought Sheetrock.

A security guardrail rose to admit them and another stood in their way a few feet along the declining cement where a folding fire door was closed. A video screen perched atop a rover rolled over to the driver's side door on tank treads and stopped to scan the individuals present in the vehicle and x-ray them.

A series of beeps indicated something was happening. They held their breath. Nothing was considered out of the ordinary. They exhaled.

Part of the mech-armor's defense system included a shield against low level x-rays and other forms of radiation that helped to hide the weaponized exoskeleton that was now a permanent part of his body. He thought back to an ancient sci-fi paperback that he had had as a kid. There was a bright blue sky and great hills of desert sand sprawled across the worn cover of the thick book. *Dune it was called*, he thought happy for the memory. *I feel like I'm wearing one of those still-suits to keep me alive. I have to learn to live like this.*

Yu held up an unfolded letter to the bot's screen. A giant eye faded to a small black dot on the metal-glass surface. A red light flashed in a line and scanned the complicated barcode series that filled the header.

"I hope this still works after last time" she whispered.

"Last time?" he growled. The tablet-sized screen gave a **click** that sounded like a film camera taking a picture and then the head of a CGI security guard appeared, complete with a cartoonish hat and badge.

"When I came here to steal your newest fashion statement."

"My what?

"Your mech-suit!" she whispered in exasperation.

"You used that same clearance letter? Are you crazy? This is the God damned central intelligence government we're talkin' about here" he said.

An OWOOGA alarm began to go off. He watched her jump in her skin next to him and immediately look around for a way out, as the noise bellowed in the tight space. Red emergency lights swirled from either side of the shadowy corridor.

Escape seemed futile, but Sheetrock knew he could fight his way out if he had to. He closed his eyes and inside his lids he could use a computer memory interface that had mapped and gridded out all of the area he had observed and recreate it in real time. He could look past corners and barriers as though he were walking around.

He came to a conclusion: in so tight a space he could only mourn for the lack of escape routes. It was doubtful he could get Yu out unhurt, if he could even get himself out. Cyber was a juggernaut.

The rover with the chrome iPad for a head backed slowly away from the van. It sent a flash of light to a scanner by a hidden door, and the round wall folded in upon itself, revealing a doorway that entered into the garage's guardhouse booth. Sheetrock stuck his head out of the window – being sure to hold the collar of his trench coat closed to hide any of the mech protruding from his chest. He heard the sound of many footsteps echoing in a stairwell.

"Someone's coming."

"Shit." Yu looked over her shoulder and saw that the first of the garage's barriers had already dropped down barring the way behind the van.

OWOOGA

"There must be a staircase to all of the garage levels off of that guard booth." But it would be filled with defenses.

There was the hum of a garage door opener and then the wall in front of them went up, disappearing into the roof. The gate started to rise and the OWOOGA continued on.

"Looks like we're in like Quinn" said Sheetrock in disbelief. Yu did not relax though and gripped the steering wheel with white knuckles and waited with bated breath for the opportunity to drive into the facility.

"HALT!" said an unseen voice. "DO NOT PROCEED. AN ESCORT IS REQUIRED."

"Jeez – us, Mary, and Mohammad" she whispered.

Her head flicked left over her shoulder and then right, but before she could even consider squeezing the paddle shifter into reverse, eight troops with B9 scatter pistols thrust forward surrounding their ride. A soldier clinked on the driver's side window with the barrel of her gun.

"I'm sorry, ma'am. There's been an attack on the drones outside. Liberal bastards, I mean political protestors, have started firing on them with illegal arms. The lower level is on lockdown for security purposes. We will allow you to park, but then we will have to escort you to the main entrance out front where a comprehensive security team is ready to keep you safe for your business as guests of the Cyber government today."

They had no choice but to roll forward into an open parking spot and follow the soldiers back up the ramp and out onto the street. Luckily the rainy gloom prevented visibility, because Sheetrock's armor came to his wrists and continually stuck out of the loose black raincoat that swirled about him in the wind. Yu squeezed his palm.

"Now you have to go in or they'll arrest you on suspicion" she said. "But stay in the lobby" she all but growled behind closed teeth.

"THEY FLY IN TOWN, THEY GET SHOT DOWN! THEY FLY IN TOWN, THEY GET SHOT DOWN!" went the chant.

A crowd approached the newcomers, instigated by the sight of their armed escort. Without warning a shot was fired and a small helidrone smashed into the sidewalk across the street where it sparked and smoked. A megaphone crackled to life.

"DISPERSE! IT IS ILLEGAL TO GATHER ON CYBER GROUNDS TO PROTEST. IT IS ILLEGAL FOR UNAUTHORIZED PERSONNEL TO HOLD FIREARMS. IT IS ILLEGAL TO DAMAGE DRONES. IT IS ILLEGAL TO DAMAGE CAMERAS. DISPERSE! IT IS ILLEGAL TO GATHER ON CYBER GROUNDS WITHOUT AUTHORIZATION. YOU HAVE ONE MINUTE BEFORE A BATTALION OF B.O.N.E.S. IS RELEASED. DISPERSE! YOU HAVE FIFTY SECONDS! DISPERSE!"

Waves of people crashed upon Yu and Sheetrock. They were not moving away from the Cyber building, but toward it. The guards tried to use the butt of their rifles to push protestors out of the way. But the people had been victims of a system that was a shell of the United States government that had run New York in the early twentieth century (before their own decline).

High above them, he could see tall sticks raised up with wine openers pressing on the trigger of spray paint canisters that were blacking out many of the shifting cameras on the nearest telephone pole. The rounded security cameras moved 360 degrees quickly and resembled gecko eyes in both their bulbousness and their ability to quickly shift and scan the area.

"DISPERSE!" went the loudspeaker.

"HELL NO, WE WON'T GO!"

"DISPERSE!" went the megaphone.

"THEY FLY IN TOWN, THEY GET SHOT DOWN!"

Yu and Sheetrock knew that the bots had been unleashed onto the crowd; but a vibrant series of screams sent shivers down their spines.

And Sheetrock did not want to be revealed. He grasped Yu by her tiny hand and used his other to swipe at anyone foolish enough to get in his way. His fingers became covered in a sharp metal skin, a mesh weave that dropped down from the forearm and created a kind of mitten with spikes on the outside, and with it he thrust aside a couple of muscle-heads with two sift jabs and one extension of his bear claw. Without the help of the overwhelmed security detail, he guided Yu inside the clear glass doors and into a massive lobby that held two pillboxes facing outside and another force of soldiers with their dog robot companions beside them.

Many chairs lined the expansive walls, as passing the main security could be difficult and time consuming; many left their coworkers outside of Cyber altogether if they could help it. She pointed to an empty chair.

"You don't understand simple gestures now, Sheetrock? Sit. I'll be back as soon as I can."

A long line stood looking nervously back at the screaming crowd as riot police cleaned up after the ruthless B.O.N.E.S. Yu walked to the end of the line and began to remove her boots and place them on the long conveyor belt that weighed, photographed, videoed, and scanned every article placed on the airport line-like entrance into the government building. Every few feet a soldier and a robot stood scrutinizing each person in the room.

Yu disappeared into the middle of the slow moving line, and Sheetrock turned to watch the melee outside. Tormented faces pressed to the glass doors in anguish, as bots and arresting officers fenced them in and pinned them down for detainment. A sound of a scattergun went off twice in a row and a mangy girl of thirty seized the moment and rushed past the occupied and distracted door sentries and the pillboxes.

Her makeshift dreadlocks hung tightly down to the base of her back and her wet, slender feet slipped on the smooth tiles. She tripped and went sprawling to the floor. And then the unarmed young lady looked up in awe of her surroundings.

Sheetrock would have said that she was beautiful if it were not for the trouble and pain that shone at the corners of her brown eyes. Deep went the marks of struggle and strife that weighed on her face. For a moment her smile glowed as she saw the bright interior of Cyber for the very first time.

Then a B.O.N.E.S. bot leaped onto her back and slammed her down into the granite floor. Her nose was bloody as she forced her head up in a snarl for vengeance. Five guards set their batons on her. Teeth, sweat, and blood flew. He looked away.

As the line moved forward, he could just see Yu as she stripped on the other side of the magnetic gate. They had let her inside. And for that, Sheetrock was grateful.

57

TORTURE

A high-pitched ZAP filled the air and ceased, but there was no bug zapper within sight. Nick Reno dialed up the juice on the battery cell again with the sharp twist of a knob. The ZAP became loud.

He dialed back on the knob and returned the small bedroom to silence. His vacant stare did not follow his hands, but instead remained fixed on her.

She knew this was where he took the children. Her children. And he liked to toy with her mind. He got off on torturing her. He constantly referred to her as a 'dirty whore of a girlfriend' even though her only offense was having had the bad fortune to have met him and been kidnapped by him four months prior. But he had never brought her in there before.

Nick looked at her with that blank stare, and in her head she thought he got a sexual thrill scanning her up and down, as she lie naked on the small bed, but his pupils were hid from her in the shadows. All she knew was that his vacant look seemed satisfied.

Her wrists and ankles were tied to the bedposts with nylon cords that dug deeply into her purpled skin. Reno had cruelly stretched and forced her legs apart so that her feet were on the outside of the posts in an unnatural split that caused her thighs to cramp and spasm. The situation itself hurt her more than the physical pain, however.

He raised two rusted alligator clips, one red and one black, and he released his tongue and very slowly licked up the sides of each of them, never taking his eyes off of his girlfriend. She felt her breath grow short. She realized that the sick bastard was going to electrocute her for his own sick amusement, as he would do to her own children.

The blank stare continued to bore into her head. His movements were swift and deliberate. But she could not get over him, could not look away. It was that frightfully empty and somehow maniacal look.

He pulled and slackened the clips' lines and dragged them over to her. He swung a leg over her waist and sat there looking at her. The weight of him sent most of the air from her lungs. He dropped the heavy alligator clips onto her ribs and leaned down and grabbed her breasts. He squeezed and tugged, and despite her best efforts, her nipples became pointed.

ZAP.

She screamed.

58

THUNDER

Riding into the thunderstorm was not like riding off into the sunset. It hurt.

Despite many internal bouts, William Waltz, often shut his mouth right when he needed to, but with Xera's stubbornness the macabre just slipped out of him. And it ruined their relationship.

Too often he was the tried and true soldier of experience and called, 'a jittery man who needs to relax' after he had walked away. He had seen too much or at least had thought too much at whatever he had seen, and most people did not like to be openly corrected, even if they were wrong.

Smooth as Waltz was, he was jittery, and he admitted it. He had the barrage of thoughts combined with bits of knowledge that swarmed his brain in ways he could not begin to understand.

This was an impulse he had little to do with. Things popped into his head and, when he could not stop them, they flew out of his mouth. Fervent pessimism surfaced in his speech with her, no matter how hard he tried not to sound conceited and abysmal or how much he declared his own allegiance to optimism (with just a touch of realism thrown in for good measure). This fault – something he worked on all the time – was the breaking point.

"I need you to clarify, please" he said hurriedly. "I am entirely in your hands, Xera. I owe you, I know I do, but I need to know."

Xera glared at him; he had only allowed her one full minute of silence to take in the beauty of the lightning before he had started up again, full-steam. He could not help it.

"I owe you a lot" he said, "and I feel terrible about what's happened." He glanced down to the bloody bandage that was the only thing keeping her thumbnail from falling from her mangled hand. Doubt and embarrassment struck with his fumbling words; he did not want to remind her that she was just tortured. And it was his fault for that.

"Then sit there quietly, watch the lightning, and trust me" she said. "We've reached a point where we have to change the game. If we don't you're going to get caught."

"I hear you, believe me, I do." Lightning flashed in a bright sequence of nearby trees in the blurred view of the car window. "But you have to tell me why exactly we're going to see someone this volatile, expensive, and dangerous."

"You really should trust me by now." He said nothing.

"The reason is because I see no other way, nowhere else to turn to" she said staring out at the dark clouds in anticipation. "He is a doctor that does DNA transfiguration and plastic surgery on the side. He has a lucrative private practice that is strictly off the books, and because he's the best at what he does, no one can touch him."

Waltz's face fell.

"What?"

"You need a new face, my friend. I'm sorry, but it's time" she answered him softly. "There's no way around that now" she said somberly. Xera seemed to pity him.

"Don't you think that's a little much? There are other ways to escape. Come on!"

"There are other ways... but you won't escape from Cyber. Their reach spans the globe and covers half the solar system, as you know better than I."

"So say goodbye to the face you know and have loved all your life! Fuck that face! You need a new one! Forget that you and I both hate the idea of implanting unnatural machines into the body! Forget it! Because the standard you've kept up your entire life – including never even dying your hair – that standard might as well have involved shooting growth hormones into your butt cheeks while breasts fell to your waist, because you're going to scrap your entire face! Scrap it!" he said.

"Stop speaking in the third person. Stop talking" said Xera. But he went on, of course.

"Alter your very own personal marker in nature – your face and your DNA – and kiss William Waltz a fond farewell! Goodbye! Fun while it lasted!"

Xera stopped the car. The lurch of the brakes and the mild whiplash did not register.

"Okay, so kiss my face goodbye. And how do you possibly expect me to not only pay you, and really well I might add, but I then pay this egotistical sociopath whatever the hell he wants? You don't have any idea what he'll want, and you expect me to believe you when you say this is going to work?" he asked. "You've got to be kidding me!" he yelled in exasperation. "It's my face!"

Thunder cracked. In the gray backdrop of the land beyond the car windows, her eyes blazed. In contrast, their brown hue sizzled around the edges and nearly took on an effect of a great log just starting to really catch in a campfire.

"There are a few clients of his that were able to talk him into taking on their cases. They agreed to a period of years of indentured servitude to cover what he did medically" she said matter-of-factly. Her patience with him waned to ebb. And so she pushed back.

"Good Christ! Years of being the guy's slave? His personal lap dog?"

"Yes. His methods are cutting edge and his own cost, his overhead, is more than you could possibly fathom, even working high up in the government like you used to do" said Xera wryly. The car bumped along in the sloshing rain. The lightning ceased for the time being.

"I bet it's bloody high!" he said, shouting. *And remind me one more time how my employer has not only fired me but is trying to have me killed*, he thought. "I am a cyber-warrior for the world's largest civilization, and you expect me to slave away for some asshole I don't even know?"

"You were a cyber-warrior."

"I'll always be a cyber-warrior! Do not ever try and take that away from me! It's bad enough you want my face. MY FACE!"

More sarcastic quips escaped his lips then, in flurries. Even his happiest of comments or past compliments to her could not begin to make up for his fierce scrutiny of her idea for his escape. He was a natural born competitor and too damn smart for his own good, and the wild words picked on her very nature as a smart secretive young woman in the prestigious role of a cyber spy. Her pride was hurt.

After the red left his vision, he was surprised to see that she did not beat on him or turn and at least shout back. She held her hands – bandages and all – into balled fists. He felt terrible all over again. This poor girl had gotten her thumbnail ripped off for him.

Waltz knew then that he should have fallen silent and just brooded over his bad luck. He would have seen through her hints and realized that his fate might be kinder than she was hinting at. But she could tell that his optimism was in short supply and was tired of it... tired of him. He had nearly gotten her killed and had successfully gotten her drugged and tortured. For him. And now he doubted her when it mattered most.

And Waltz knew as soon as he had spoken that he should have just let it alone and not offered a commentary of what his internal monologue played (and should have remained internal). Finally, after what seemed like an hour, she did not turn but she reacted; Xera cleared her throat quietly so that when she spoke the words would emerge and she would only have to say them once.

"Fine. I guess you have all the answers then" she said. "You know where to go, right?" The car's engine chugged softly amidst the falling rain along the side of the muddy road. Waltz's grumbling stopped and a precognitive pang of fear tweaked in his chest. "You going to drive?" Xera asked in a voice that mocked a submissive southern bell.

He got out slamming the door as he went. No sooner had he stepped away than she threw the car into gear and peeled away into the night. After all, her life was at stake too.

59

POLITICAL PROTEST

The guns protruding from the slit in the pillboxes moved slowly and assuredly. Their greasy black barrels remained fixed on the throngs of protestors that amassed near the building's front doors. The cries began to outweigh the shouts. Sheetrock tried to sit as normally as someone who was actually alarmed at the nearby chaos and human brutality.

He was alarmed too. But this feeling did not come from the melee outside. It came from sitting in the lobby of Cyber's New York headquarters while wearing their stolen multimillion dollar weaponized Mech-suit. He had never heard of any type of exo-suit being removed from a living person's body, and if they wanted his armor back, there could be a conflict of interests.

If only the black market transactions came with receipts and no return policies, he thought sarcastically.

An elevator at the far end of the lobby opened its steel doors and a dozen infantry trotted out in two single file lines. They marched straight to the security gate and spread out along the wall with the other soldiers stationed there.

What now? thought Sheetrock. His forehead began to sweat, despite the temperature-controlled armor keeping his body comfortable. *Maybe they're just changing shifts.*

More men and women on Cyber business trickled in from the street, despite the ongoing commotion and violent outbreaks in front of the building. Most appeared to either be business people, stock market zombies, or administrative employees of Cyber.

He glanced up and down the room and looked to Yu while also counting the bolstered security force. He closed his eyes and let the digital mapping take over. Brightened figures made exploring his options in the massive room far easier.

There were two B.O.N.E.S. bots sniffing out his section of the lobby, while four of their controllers watched the front of the building and him; two stood right behind the pillboxes to his left and two were on his side of the security gate facing the glass doors. On the side furthest from him, there were twenty-four guards and four door wardens checking in the line of people attempting to properly enter into the facility.

Sheetrock opened his eyes and raised his slumped head. He was caught between pillboxes and a battalion that was right on top of him. They would not let him get so far as the line to enter. He read it in their eyes. After all, he was an outsider and had to wait for his verified companion to return.

The thought ripped through him: *I'm trapped. There's no in or out if Yu doesn't get it done.*

New shouts struck him. It was different this time. The hurried calls inside did not blend in with the general protestor babble that he had listened to for the last hour plus. There were directed military commands spoken, in code, back and forth amidst the clamor.

The units behind the pillboxes hustled away to find the doors to their secure bunkers; the creepy robotic dogs turned and went with them. Sheetrock looked back and all of the soldiers by the gates stood tense and alert. They were anticipating something wicked that approached. He could see it in their faces.

"God, what now?" he asked aloud to himself or his maker. And as if that was the password, the barred glass doors at the front of the lobby burst open. Bodies of all shapes, of all ages, of all genders, of long natty hair and short spiky hair, and expensive custom made suits and dresses or ragged jeans that dragged on the floor – they all rushed forward and crammed into the tight space between the pillboxes.

Sheetrock was convinced that most of them would be mowed down and was surprised when none of the daring demonstrators even gave so much as a cautious glimpse at the defenses. But the people knew better than he did. The impenetrable doors would not have opened if the government did not allow them to enter; they would not be cut down so swiftly and painfully and publically like that. Or so they thought.

"CITIZENS, THIS IS A WARNING! DISPERSE! RETREAT OR PREPARE TO BE TAKEN DOWN WITH LETHAL FORCE! DISPERSE!" went the loudspeakers. This surprised Sheetrock as much as it did the crowd.

"Come on, people" whispered Sheetrock, as he climbed to his feet with his hands held palm outward.

What did the dozens of runners see? Once they got past the pillboxes, the floor was open and huge; the ceiling was fifty feet or higher above their heads, and only one man stood before the walls of the security gates.

"You don't have to do this" he said. "Please just get out of here before they do something to."

His plea to the throng was cut short, as a trio of teenagers – he could not tell if they were guys or girls or neither – hit him with part of a defunct android carcass and sent him sprawling. As he climbed back to his feet, the teens threw themselves at him with their keys held tightly in their hands stabbing at his coat.

Before he could push the kids back, a pale bald man of enormous height and girth cracked him on the back of the neck with two hands clenched tightly together. Joseph Estol was there to make newspaper headlines. He knew that infiltrating Cyber would do just that, and he had six members of the media tuning in to his camera feed as it recorded from his belt live.

Sheetrock's back was still tender from the installation procedure, and it felt like he had been beaten like railroad spikes. His thoughts reached out to connect with every part of his body, from extremity to extremity to brainstem and back. Then he bulked up his hands with the suit's spiked overlays. Beneath the start of his heels, a piece surrounded his feet inside the boots and grew there until the footwear burst open revealing a tightly wound covering that was littered with an enforced material topped with small spikes; the blows would not hurt him but would slice into the enemies.

Without a thought, he brought a plated kneecap up into the bald man's midsection. Joseph slumped a little but was not slowed down. The bear of a man sent an uppercut to Sheetrock's jaw that would have broken it if the mech-armor exoskeleton had not climbed up his neck and lips, supporting him far more than the human body was capable of. The teenagers grappling with his lower body actually helped to keep him upright too.

Jonah, Missy, and Danny thirsted for adventure and their intelligence combined with their adolescence made them ripe for the anti-government movement; what they did not realize until they were caught up in crowd-thought was that their subconscious held an aggression that hungered for violence so strongly that it was almost involuntary.

The three teenagers screeched in tones, like birds warning predators away from a nest of their children, as they tore at Sheetrock's feet trying to trip him. By this time the overflow of the crowd pushed up to the lobby's gates and many of those swarmed around him for no other reason than that was what everyone else was doing. But they could not deal many blows, because of their fellow supporters.

The giant Joseph brushed the sweat off of the top of his head and grimaced. He pounded at Sheetrock with his two massive arms, and swung wildly and danced about in a circle, like a boxer, forcing the other demonstrators to give the tangled quintet some room to brawl.

Sheetrock did the best he could to ward off the powerful fists and forearms, but the kids held onto his legs and limited his movements. All he could do was bob his head and use his own hands to soften the hits. It was not enough though. When Joseph missed an uppercut meant to appear as a knockout punch, a feint, his right fist slammed down onto the top of Sheetrock's spinal column.

This sent excruciating pain through Sheetrock, the like of which he had never known. He thought he would die right there on the tiled floor looking down at the multitude of feet and the three brats that clung to him tightly, biting and clawing (though not getting through the tough skin he wore). The agony burned his entire spine and tidal waves spread throughout his nervous system.

"Aaarrrhh!" he howled.

Without knowing how he did it, a long triangular piece of carbon blade protruded from the knees of the Mech-suit. Fury blinded him and the digital outlines of each person in the room blazed and then dissipated in his vision.

Sheetrock took two large steps up and forward, and the bone protrusions – sharp as razors – cut neatly into Missy and Danny as his knees lifted. Their cries quickly became gurgles, and they fell in bloody clumps to the floor. Jonah dove back into the crowd wailing hysterically.

Sheetrock was tackled to the floor. Joseph's walrus mustache twitched while he beat the space captain's chest and face. His back stiffened with each blow.

Technically, Sheetrock was still in the pupal stage. He did not know it at the time, but the adrenaline and the rage were able to begin the armor's bio-hardening and strengthening processes. And that was a lucky thing.

In a smooth, fluid motion, he sent two locked hands forward and forced Joseph off balance. Sheetrock had been in many fights, and he sprang down on Joseph and sent a blow that shattered the bridge of the nose and sent blood gushing.

The crowd screamed in surprise and returned to the fight. Sheetrock warded as many of the blows as he could and found himself in a compelled state of motion. He used to grumble when he had to get up to get the remote for watching the TV, but he found a new quickness he had never known was possible.

The suit also gave him flexibility. He swiftly tore through the people, targeting vital arteries that were highlighted in bright red on his digital vision. He sliced at each vessel with a jagged triangular extension from his hands and knees and easily opened their veins.

It was over within four or five minutes. The doors to the outside had shut. Once the crowd no longer received support from growing numbers, Sheetrock spun, sliced, rolled, sliced, and bobbed and weaved and sliced until the whole lot of them was maimed badly or dead on the floor.

When the crowd stopped coming at him, he stood still and caught his breath. The digital borders faded to real-world granite and tile in the lobby. Sheetrock breathed deeply. He was exhausted and in terrible pain.

And then he heard the soft sound of clapping come from the elevators across the room and saw that his tattered coat's remains rested not on his body but on the floor. He stood there as the guards stared open mouthed at the Cyber mech-armor.

60

PRECARIOUS

Oh God! Sheetrock's thoughts screamed within his head. *I have to get out! They know it's theirs! They'll kill me for this!* But he cocked his head and what he heard caused him to stop and reassess the situation. Golden and ruby outlines crept back into view defining the walls and the people in the main room with him.

The applause came as such a surprise that Sheetrock turned toward the pillboxes and front doors without a second glance. With a long stride he dropped the nearest demonstrator that had crawled to his feet and was nearing the gap in the two fortifications when he heard a familiar voice.

"Stop!" yelled Fae Yu. And then he could not be sure what her small voice uttered after that, because it was lost in the cavernous hall. He thought she said, "It's okay! Sheetrock, it's okay." But he could not be sure.

Sheetrock stepped out of a tangle of bodies carefully. It brought the situation home to him.

"What the fuck did I just do?" he asked mortified. Murdering was not an action he had ever taken to before that day, even in self-defense. He had violated one of Moses's sacred commandments and shaken his religious foundation to its stone foundation. There were cracks in it. What choice had God given him in any of this?

The furious feelings remained strong, burning throughout his limbs, especially after the violence that had been forced upon him. He continued to read thermal marks of Cyber guards in the immediate vicinity. It was a darkened vision of the complex. The outlines of each wall and room became faintly glowing geometric shapes of varying reds and yellows and blues.

What was invisible to the naked eye – and even the bionic eye replacements – was accessible to Sheetrock. As reinforcements crept into the pillboxes from underground trapdoors, and a protective electrical field formed a wall inside the lobby's front doors, he saw them. Each emitted unique heat signatures that stood out bright pink and fire-orange amidst the black, lightless background that the Mech-suit offered to the sensors accepting messages from his optic nerves.

He had no idea what being electrocuted in the armor would do to him, and he had confirmed Yu's personal signature from across the lobby. He could not abandon her with all she had done for him, even if it meant he would die as the government took back their property. With a grunt, he turned back and headed toward the conveyor belts and the walls of security gates and personnel.

"Wait!" cried Yu. "Don't try to go through the gates! I'm coming to you" she said. Sheetrock watched as she jogged to the great barriers and was admitted to pass. Another person followed quickly behind her. Their coloration in the abstract field of vision was colder than Yu's.

"I want you to relax, Sheetrock." She held up a packet and shook it in triumph. He could not make out anything on the black pages.

"Why can't I read it?" he asked. She looked concerned as she handed him the contract and even at a close distance he could not tell if there was any writing on it at all.

"It's a contract for employment. Cyber has agreed to everything we could've asked for."

"I can't see right." Sheetrock turned and looked out of the front of the building's glass; dark blue rain fell in strings to the ground outside. "I think I started some kind of sensory vision thing... an abstract field?

"You're going to have to turn that off" said the person that had followed Yu into the lobby.

"How do I do that?"

"That's a matter for your mind I'm afraid, Mr. Sheetrock. You seem to have triggered many of the suit's abilities on your own. Now you have to will the electrical signals to stop before they reach the receptors in your brain that interpret and cope with sight." The voice was clear and distant with a touch of coldness about it, or disinterestedness.

"I take it that's easier said than done."

"Our test subjects trained for eight months to be able to do just that. But, then again, not one of them survived the installation process, so the relevance of this is suspect" said Ro.

He closed his eyes tightly and the grids of architectural patterns and the heat signatures of everything remained in view. With a deep breath, he could feel the shooting pain enter his back in the areas surrounding his spine. He focused on the agonizing areas while he kept the breath in his gut. He pictured massive power lines, as thick as his closed fists that were cut before they could connect to a power source. Sheetrock exhaled and doubled over as sharp pains waxed.

The connection broke. He could see the brightly lit government headquarters and the person that stood erect and in a black pinstriped suit.

"I bet that's better."

"Yes"he said gruffly. "Let's cut to it, alright? I can tell you're an important person around here, so what exactly do you want with me?"he asked.

"My name is Ro, and I helped to invent what you are now wearing, though I would never admit to that fact outside this building."

Yu bit her lip, concerned with Sheetrock's control over the exoskeleton. Ro was a head taller than Yu and carried an air of confidence and serenity that rang alarms in his head. Ro was definitely one of the few cyber-warriors, and was more dangerous than anyone they had ever met.

The guards returned to their posts as a few others came and escorted each of the maimed bodies out to the sidewalk where a pair of ambulances waited with their lights cascading. A maintenance crew began to make piles of the deceased and mop up the syrupy pools on the wet floor tiles.

"Let's step over here out of the way" said Ro. "And I'd like you to take off that coat please, Mr. Sheetrock."

"You can stop with the commands right now. I don't know you from a hole in the wall and unless you want to actually become a part of a new hole in a wall here, I suggest you"

In a swift blur, Ro unfurled a butterfly knife and sliced and ducked beneath his reeling arms. The trench coat fell to the floor in tatters. The speed was dizzying.

"You've got one too?" Yu asked dumbfounded.

"No." Ro smiled and tapped the knife's hilt.

"This is the job for you" said Ro. "There's a high speed pursuit going on right now. So without interviewing you further, I am going to ask you three questions because we're out of time: How do you feel about hunting down a known terrorist and a murderer turned fugitive? How do you feel about a two million dollar tax-free paycheck from the government? And how do you feel about vacationing on Long Island?"

"I'm going to need a new coat."

61

STUPID

"No fucking way! No fucking way!" William Waltz shouted at the car shrinking down the rain-spattered highway. He was about to utter a last question at Xera – *What the fuck?* most likely – but a group of drones burst from the nearest tree line and sped toward the car, like metallic kites taken by a gust of wind. They had not even seen him.

In a single moment, the selfishness and stupidity of his actions came fully home to him. He had driven away his one and only ally and someone whose trust had been earned multiple times over already. And he had put her, his only companion, in mortal danger. *NO!* his thoughts screamed.

But Waltz did not crumble and instead turned up the road at a run. Instinctual focus honed his thoughts to their core. *I need a car now* was what processed.

In a world where apathy was a luxury revered and worshipped, he rarely fell into such purgatorial behavior. All of the guilt and grief of the situation confronting them was instantaneously swallowed. Forgotten.

He searched for an unguarded vehicle – preferably an older one – that he could quickly hotwire and use to chase after Xera and the four helidrones before they hunted her down. And there it was. Sitting in mud up to the door panels. A beat up boat of a car.

As Waltz strode into the tall grass, he assumed the maroon sedan would be long dead. Despite the rain and the situation, his curiosity got the better of him and he glanced at the inspection sticker on the windshield and read that the faded boat (that was the color of dried blood) was actually a 1985 Lincoln Town Car. He had never heard of Lincoln before unless it was in reference to the long-dead United States president of yore.

The heavy door opened with a tug across the mud and he launched himself inside. The door closed tightly and the howl of the wind and the storm was immediately muffled to a dull murmur on the car's ceiling. As he sat back, it was the most confortable leather seat he had ever touched.

The sun visor was flipped down impeding a full view, and Waltz thought this odd but did not have time to register it. He thrust a hand upward and flicked back the visor, and a key that had been tied to the shield by a rubber band fell into his lap.

"You've got to be kidding me" he said in disbelief. "There's no way this thing's going to work."

As the long key bottomed out in the steering column, he turned the ignition and let out a yelp of surprise as a low sound of flooding brought the fuel injectors and the motor in sync, and the Lincoln fired up. To say that a miracle had just taken place would be an understatement. Someone had kept this dented boat alive for nearly a hundred years.

With a grim laugh, he put the car in gear, spun the tires furiously, and with a fishtailing of epic proportions swung the huge car over the wet grass and onto the road. The Lincoln's tires gripped the pavement hard and rocked the beast forward and Waltz soared off toward Xera and the pursuing drones. The engine quickly roared and sent him further back against his seat as the speed picked up dramatically.

* * *

Sunrise Highway came up just before Waltz was catching up Xera. He watched her skip the red traffic light that was guarding the entrance to the highway. A truck passing through its own green light was about to rear-end Xera's Mini when one of the drones, thrown by the simple light-hopping maneuver, hit into the truck's windshield. The pickup slammed on its brakes and avoided hitting Xera, as it swerved and went off the road. The drone broke into fragments on contact.

Three helidrones remained. They continued to close on the Mini as it pulled onto Sunrise and picked up speed. The straight away allowed her to accelerate to eighty miles per hour without worry of anything but the three robotic units firing some kind of sharp dart-like round at her tires. She veered left and right, careful not to slide too much in the rain and lose control of the vehicle, but the drones swooped in and would get near enough to take out her wheels in seconds.

A fit of honking lunacy shook the air. Waltz was all over the road but managed to get the Lincoln up to eighty and right onto the Mini's ass. The nearest drone flew straight up in surprise and the other two scattered in opposite directions. The disruption had interrupted the bots' flow and they did not have the horsepower to be able to catch up, quickly, once their momentum was disrupted. The drones were gone.

Unfortunately, sirens went up shrilly. Backup had arrived.

62

PURSUIT

The New York Cyber Police (NYCP) monitored all of the Long Island skies and roads via cross-satellite fields, like distant nets covering the earth. Once the Cyber drones had visual confirmation of the fugitive Waltz, and his compatriot, they had alerted the local authorities to set up a roadblock and standby as backup. But the command could not be carried out.

The pursued, William Waltz, had apparently split up with his partner in the Mini Cooper, an as yet unidentified female of age approximately twenty-five to thirty years, and begun to drive his own car, an ancient 1985 Lincoln Town Car. After a disruption in the pursuit, the two of them proceeded onto Sunrise Highway before the exit could be barricaded.

There were a series of HONKS as cars avoided the newcomers that drove down the onramp and onto the roadway at great speed. Oddly enough, the two cars stayed tightly together in a single-file formation. All forces were concentrated on the pair and remained back but within sight of the pursued.

Blocking the highway was not an option, as it would endanger too many lives. People – especially Long Island drivers – would not be able to stop or be rerouted or even comprehend in time in the rain. The car chase was dangerous enough and local snails and speed demons alike were bound to get hurt as the NYCPD assisted Cyber in attaining the suspects.

63

HONK

In an unlikely strategy, Waltz did not part ways and continued to follow Xera closely. The two cars kept to a strict limit of eighty-five miles per hour in the steady dark. They did not want to hydroplane and do flips.

Separating might have lured the authorities away from her, but he did not think so; Cyber was too invested in stopping one of their own, and they would do anything, including learning all they could from Xera now that she was out in the open. The more he thought about it, the more he was sure that 'the powers that be' had become extremely interested in her. He put on a favorite grunge-punk album from the last century (when real music had been made and real sound had been recorded onto analog, and not the flat, talentless digital contemporary star "musicians").

Luckily the slick road was not packed with cars at that time of night, as the curfew was in full effect. There were still pockets of traffic that refused to budge when they drew up behind them. A driver shifted over without looking to see who was also in the lane and cutoff Waltz. The gas-guzzling hybrid Expedition was three times the length and twice the width and height of Xera's Mini, and yet the Cadillac slid over in between he and Xera and by some freak chance of physics did not so much as graze either vehicle.

Waltz slammed on the brakes to avoid hitting the colossal tank on the highway and felt the backend of the Lincoln start to go out. His car was a boat with wheels; though when put next to the black Caddy, the Town Car was smaller in every way. He mastered the floating rear end in time to nearly be run into by a police car that was not paying close attention.

HONK HONK

More bystanders driving without a clue as to what was going on in their surroundings honked as they either sped faster or slowed and moved around the pursued and their entourage. The many storefronts on Sunrise were broken and their signs had letters that no longer illuminated, like Spo_t_ Authority and Pet_o.

The early spring night felt more like a late winter eve for all of the dimness that accompanied the flurries of rain and wind.

"Shit!" said Waltz, as he egged the car to go faster. He did not floor the gas pedal, because he would have lost control in the rain, and though the 5.0-liter engine had Mustang power it was still slow in the acceleration department due to the enormous ass it was handling.

Slowly the speedometer needle floated around the midnight mark and over the eighty line. The cop backed off. HONK HONK HONK

"Up yours!" Waltz shouted in retaliation (to no one in particular).

I wonder what Xera's thinking right about now. Then he remembered how she was pissed at him and would be until he apologized profusely.

We can't stay out here with all of these meatheads in SUV's; we're liable to get killed, he thought.

The Mini Cooper shimmied a little as it got over into the right lane and then exited Sunrise Highway for the Southern State Parkway. He followed. The police did too.

"Yes, Xera, yes! That's it, girl!" he screamed and hooted for joy – which was entirely out of character for him, but somehow felt absolutely necessary in that place and moment.

There was a chance that the cops had outsmarted them, had anticipated their move and had already headed them off toward a roadblock and road spikes that they could not pass and live. It was a chance they had to take though, and it seemed Xera was well aware of this fact. The highway could bring them to Ocean Parkway quickly, and if they achieved that golden road then there would be very few cars on it at all.

The winding wooded parkway was treacherous in the rain, especially nearing a hundred miles per hour, but the Southern State was a means to an end. If they reached Ocean Parkway and on to Jones Beach, there would be plenty of opportunities to lose the cars and approach the dunes on foot. There were boats everywhere along the narrow strip of island and since the rain had bloomed there would be little or no traffic heading out to the ocean beaches or the concert venue.

64

SLIPPERY

As the Southern State rolled on, so did the music. Heavy drumbeats mixed with roaring guitars and a one of a kind voice that filled the cab of the Lincoln. The sound had an emotional ferocity that reverberated with his ears, the peeling sides of the car, and his soul. The police became a distant string of round headlights in William Waltz's rearview mirror. He noted Xera ahead of him and continued to head bang, wishing he did not have such short hair at that instant.

From out of the shadows of the trees two state troopers crept up and rolled into the side of each of their cars. They had kept their lights off and sped onto the parkway from the grassy shoulders. The rain was lighter but a fog emerged to cloud the waters.

"NO!" Waltz jerked the wheel back toward the left where he had been hit to avoid being spun around. He collided lightly with the cop car again and jiggled the steering wheel to straighten out the Lincoln and maintain control. All of his mind was bent on looking forward in the direction he wanted to go, while staying on the gas and feeling for the right amount of pressure to keep the rubber gripping on the road.

Xera too was hit and she fishtailed and nearly lost it. But she had also trained in adverse driving conditions. The cyber-warrior kept control and gave the Mini a lot of gas and shot forward, like a cannonball. The trooper had not anticipated such resilience. He was left behind.

"Time to fuck you all up" said Waltz. He pushed the Town Car's pedal to the floor, risking death by hydroplaning. The rotting maroon car chugged loudly and pushed forward past the trooper and then drove up to the back bumper of her trooper's car. The Lincoln nudged the cop car and sent it off to the shoulder where it slid up a small hillock and stopped; the troopers within were unharmed, though they would need new uniform pants.

The pair of outlaws drove on at a hundred until the Ocean Parkway exit. There they slowed to a modest forty miles per hour and successfully exited the Southern State. No roadblock waited and the drones were nowhere to be seen. But Cyber was far from giving up on catching them.

65

REDEMPTION

"Something's not right."

But Xera Finn looked back and saw her 'client' William trailing closely behind her. *I'm only going to get rich off of my dumb ass 'client'* she thought, *if he doesn't get himself killed in that freaking boat of his.* She was still steaming.

The truth was she was glad that Waltz had returned, though she would never admit it to him. He had been just in time to save her from the helidrones. They would have run her off the road if not for him and his heap of a car. But he was also trouble the like of which she had never imagined possible. And he dragged with him a long line of police cars in hot pursuit. She turned the volume up on Amanda Palmer's blaring punk cabaret.

The rain glistened with the bright red lights that leapt from their vehicles. Xera pushed just over a hundred to get a little more distance between them and the cops. The green grasses were not long enough to hide the ocean and the bay on either side of the narrow parkway; the long arms of water stretched out for the road and flooded many pockets in the plains.

At least with the empty road ahead she felt her taut muscles relax a little in her forearms. The steering wheel was loose in her fingers. Her mind pulsed at a more pleasant rate and thoughts were easier to decipher.

The line of cars curved back and forth behind her on the flat parkway blinking, like hanging strands of

Christmas lights. They kept their steady distance. *It's going to work*, she thought.

But she could not let go of the pit in her stomach. The relaxation of her hands was one thing, but the muscles from her waist down were practically cramped up and her ankles were extremely tight from holding the gas pedal down to maintain speed. She could not shake the feeling that something was wrong or foreboding, even as she gained a larger distance from the police.

"Where the hell am I going to go?" she asked aloud. *Would it be better to pull away and get off the road now? Traverse the dunes. Or would it be better to get nearer to Jones Beach and get lost in the massive lots over there?*

She did not know if waiting for Jones Beach was merely a way to delay the hard race on foot in the rain with the NYCPD, their swift canines, and the Cyber agents (with B.O.N.E.S. in tow) chasing closely behind. Fleeing was not something that Xera was used to. She pursued, she hid, she observed, she attacked, but she was always active as opposed to passively retreating and hoping for escape.

The realization of this, a reaffirmation of sorts, made the decision for her. Xera had to take control of the situation that had gotten too far away from her steering. The whole thing had to be turned on its head before it was too late. The ancient Lincoln's engine could blow up at any time.

The Mini accelerated. In seconds the one hundred became one hundred and fifteen miles per hour. She bit her lip as she watched Waltz catch up to her (gritting his teeth). There was only seconds to give them an edge.

The rain swept across the Lincoln's bow harder than it had been in an hour but still the old beast pushed forward. She waited until he was right on her bumper and then held her breath. As she had anticipated the cops had been in a bit of a lull, perhaps waiting for backup to come on them at unawares from the west, and so they completely lost view of them.

She turned off her headlights so that the police would not see a trace of her leaving the road. A wide but gradual decline of grass and high tide bushes went out in a stretch before a rise of trees and dunes to the west, and Xera hit her brake, and the second she dropped to forty, turned and greeted the foliage. Miraculously, the slick surface of the rain helped her over the line of hedge without losing the car.

"YES!" she yelled joyfully.

In a matter of seconds she heaved in her breath and slowed the Mini to a crawl underneath the thick cover of the marsh-like brush. She had squiggled all over the flooding ground but had kept the car going forward until the trees were too thick to continue. She stopped.

"Oh no, William" she said. But the boat of a Town Car pulled up beside her, its hood steaming; it was so dark and raining hard enough that when he turned off the engine she had lost sight and forgotten him in the feverish attempt to hide without flipping the car. Steam clouds and fluid seeped from his car to the saturated ground.

Her body's muscles flexed and unflexed. Adrenaline lifted her body, mind, and soul. Xera waited. *Did they see us?*

The seconds passed in agony. *They saw us. They know.*

But then the long cylindrical beams of light marked the first of their pursuers. The line of police cars passed bye, over the course of ten seconds, and was gone. They had lost them. But Xera's stomach still remained clenched in worry.

66

ONLINE

One by one the brain's machine implants fired up. The implants sent signals to transceivers and relays that wirelessly linked Sheetrock's brain to the mech-armor's CPU processor. He had full control over the vastly intricate computer system and exoskeleton, and after Ro had given Sheetrock a brief summary of each of his new tools, Yu looked on as he felt the newest parts of his body turn on and off at will.

The Jeep lurched and rocked with the bumpy dunes. The downpour made the windshield a canvas of grays wiped with an influx of bubbling drops over all. But they did not have to see clearly, because they knew the short stretch of land where the fugitives had to have taken off. The NYCPD had narrowed it down; they were good for that at least.

* * *

The brain-machine interfaces (BMI) were not part of the process for adopting Sheetrock's radical life alteration, but Fae Yu made them a part of it. She had neglected to explain the details of the BMI to Sheetrock for fear that he might worry overmuch about the extraneous electrical signals that tapped his brain to send and receive data. The Mech-suit was supposed to rely on signals through the spine, but she felt that might not be direct enough. The signal might be too weak.

While he struggled with the suit's painful merge with his spine and epidermis, she strapped him down and did the necessary drilling. The CMOS chips were injected into the cortex where the neural dust settled and picked up on his brain's data, converted it, and sent it ultrasonically to the subdural transceiver that in turn relayed the dust's interpretations and data to the external transceiver attached to the skull in four places. She suspected the extra step saved his life, but she would take that secret to her grave.

* * *

The Jeep teetered for a moment and regained a flatter footing in time to prevent its rolling over in the wet sand. The sound of the transmission groaned loudly as the thirty-inch wheels churned over the difficult terrain. Sheetrock was silent, concentrated on his driving (both his own body and the vehicle).

As they left Cyber, Ro had tucked a small data drive into Yu's hands with a wink. While Sheetrock drove, she accessed her computer and pulled up the proper schematics, system specifications, and detailed instructions on how to use the numerous functions of the mech-armor. The more Yu read about the abilities – the infrared heat sensing, the hidden EMP deflector, and the architectural mapping – the more she wondered whether or not the former drill captain could handle the newer, more expanded, strain on his thought's processes.

The Jeep stopped. The ocean licked and spit at the sand twenty yards away.

"Are they here?" asked Yu.

"Yes" said Sheetrock. "They're mine." His tone was so black that she trembled as he unbuckled his seatbelt.

The wind shook the soft roof and screamed in the drafty crevices by the doors. She could not get warm.

"If I do not make it back in fifteen minutes I want you to call in the Cyber drones and the troop that's standing by." He gave her a light squeeze on the shoulder, a longtime touch of affection for his unofficial girlfriend (and life companion perhaps) and was gone into the spray and bellowing ocean breath.

"Love" she whispered to the closing door. Yu turned up the knob for the heat and peered through the gray drops.

A tiny flash of yellow brightened the night sky and the upturned beach. The waves were choppy walls of foam and then were gone. Another couple of brief flashes brought the cove back into view briefly. Yu rubbed her hands together and blew on them. She did not like the assignment; their first Cyber job should have been much easier so that Sheetrock could get acclimated to the suit. As it was, it could take months of training for him to fully harness the mech-armor's potential and properly utilize its many life functions.

A heavy figure crashed into the driver's side door and slid to the ground. A large hand rose up and then dropped to the door handle to regain balance. It was Sheetrock. She saw him get back to his feet holding his ribs and gasping for air, his shredded coat bobbing on the wind.

He looked back at her and raised his hand. From it Yu saw shining pieces of metal glint in the glow of the headlights. She gasped. *Had the armor just absorbed the scatter pistol rounds and spit them back out?*

The flash erupted, a burst of yellow gun flame, but Sheetrock had already rolled away from the Jeep and into a thick patch of dead Spikerush tussocks. Yu ducked below the dashboard and crawled into the backseat where she hid under a blanket to avoid anyone knowing she was part of the hunt.

There were night vision cameras mounted to each side of the all-terrain vehicle and with her laptop Yu was able to monitor some of the surroundings and the firefight. A burst of thunder and light flew from the reeds and scrub bushes where Sheetrock sat. The gunfire that was advancing on him from across the dunes ceased blasting and paused in the smoky blackness and blistering rain.

They were armed. Two of the Cyber guards had offered up government-issued B9 scatter pistols in brand new cases – the insides of which were lined with rounds – to the newest government employees, Yu and Sheetrock; the guns came fully loaded with advanced stabilization cylinders, mini-scopes, and armor-piercing ammunition. She cradled hers in between her ankles hoping that she would not need to use it like he was. Her orders were to let him engage the enemy – she was just the recorder.

Her five-foot tall, lean, body was on its side, under the black blanket, taut and ready to spring forward without notice. The rain collided THLAP THLAP THLAP on the soft roof loudly. The smell of gunpowder seeped into the vehicle's cabin and was rank. She wondered at the 'dead or alive' instructions they had received.

67

DAMNED IF YOU DO, DAMNED IF YOU DON'T

The coastal fields were almost completely under water. Xera Finn did not say a word to Waltz about his being an ass or his coming to her rescue. Which was *probably for the best*, he thought.

Instead, she handed Waltz a scatter pistol and strode forward into the swampy underbrush. She checked the clip and reloaded her own and looked about in either direction for any indication that they had been seen. Somewhere the satellites' imagery of the beach terrain was being directed to bunkers on the ground and drones in the air. The B.O.N.E.S. would be close behind, sniffing them out. *Thank God for the rain that often disrupted the bots' vision systems.*

When Waltz started to open his mouth, Xera put a finger over her lips and dashed off in a zigzag pattern beneath the trees. The dunes and the ocean were close, but she brought him back in the direction they had come, east, hoping to throw off the police, at least for a little while. Escape would only be ensured if they could get to a small watercraft and leave the state undetected.

After a few silent minutes, she brought them out of the woods to check to see if there was a pier nearby. They skittered along the dunes and found nothing but the black and blue wall that was the horizon and the roaring ocean and more rain. The air was freezing and smelled of salt and dead things.

He was lucky and grateful that she was still helping him. The bandage over her thumb was crimson and her gait was unsteady at times from exhaustion. *I owe her more than I'll ever be able to repay*, thought Waltz miserably.

"These are not B8's"said Xera. "They're B3's."

"I know" he whispered beside her. He knew the defect inherent in the B3's, just as he knew how much more powerful their blast was (twice as strong as the newest government-issued B9 scatter pistol). But he did not want to doubt her and would gladly take the B3 kickback of rounds (firing back and slicing into his own arms) than try and question her reasons aloud.

"I have a friend – well, sort of – his name's Carl, and he helps me track down the B3 units that weren't destroyed and buys them for me" she said.

"Really?" He was curious. Not only was the illegal gun trade punishable by death, but when they hit, the B3's could rupture most body armor in the field from a great distance.

"Yep! He has a process for modifying the chambers so that they keep their blast radius and do not lose their accuracy while cutting out the defect that grounded the guns. I have a small arsenal of them" she said. "And my guess would be that Carl probably does too." The image of Carl standing in his garage surrounded by machines and Gatling guns mounted on the tattered walls, and stacks of pistols of every shape and size on rusted benches, and wearing only tighy-whities and a deep laugh, with twists of his bushy mustache, was too hard to keep out of her mind.

She laughed as though the raging storm, the boisterous sea, and the biting wind had not enveloped them in a fisherman's net that the Cyber authorities were slowly reeling in on the sands of Jones Beach. It was beautiful and disarming.

Waltz realized he would do anything for this woman. The curves were hidden beneath her long black coat but they were still there in his mind's eye. She had it all: beauty, grace, bright smarts, an attuned moral compass, and a fierce tenacity.

UUURRRRNNNNN

The sound came as if in response to the laughter and the breaking of their silence. Something was driving among the dunes. They could not see any headlights, but someone was ballsy enough to tread the quagmire without seeing, and they probably had a hard-on for Waltz and Xera. They looked at each other and ran for the cover of the wood.

68

ALONG THE SHORE

Deeper they hiked, shivering, under the cover of the dark, dripping boughs. The wind came off of the water in gusts and penetrated the patches of wood; it had laid claim to the narrow region, the strip of barrier island, and the wind chill dropped the temperature twenty-plus degrees.

"We can ignore the cold, but it's going to affect our ability to move and fight before long" said William Waltz. He was humble, at times, and it surprised Xera.

"You have the training and the discipline of a Tibetan monk that can sit in a twenty degree room and heat a sheet soaked in freezing water with his naked body" she said. "I appreciate your concern though. I am injured. My week of sleepless nights prior to all this is" she paused.

"We have to make a run for it – find the closest boat on the shore and hope there's enough gas to at least get to New Jersey – or we have to stand and fight through whoever is out there now."

Waltz seemed to think for a minute. Despite his own injuries, he had proven the ability to suppress them, and he was driven. He was not friendless anymore. He had come back to save her from the helidrones. He had come back for her. They could go on offense... or they could fall... together.

Xera removed the gun's safety and looked through its sights. She handed him a small leather case filled with EMP grenades and made up his mind for him. She dropped her duffel bag and twirled the pistol in her palm, like a gunslinger.

"Let's go break their vaginas" she said with a nod toward the beach.

* * *

UUURRRRNNNNN

The sound of the Jeep's engine and transmission came closer. Xera could see the outline of it on top of the furthest dune up ahead. Without waiting or warning, Waltz knelt amongst a patch of shrubbery, stalked forward, and fired steadily at the driver side door that had swung open soundlessly.

She heard the grunt as Waltz hit the target. *Damn his eyes are good!* And she started firing when he paused to reload, so that the driver was unsure if there were two shooters or just one with an auto-loading ammo attachment.

The driver's position changed as bright orange light illuminated a patch of bushes near to the Jeep. The driver fired back from a partially covered position, but did not come anywhere near to them. No gun would have the power required for the distance and accuracy, except the modified B3 and she did not think it likely that whoever Cyber had sent to find them would be armed with contraband such as that.

Stooping low, Waltz broke into a trot. He zigzagged to avoid the gunfire and she followed doing the same. To their right, the black ocean was loud in its wrath and the rain that pelted the surface incessantly gave the tumultuous water goose bumps. A piece of driftwood got caught between Xera's feet and she fell to the sand with her gun to her waist knocking the wind from her.

69

THE SHELL

He knew that one good round had hit whomever it was that Cyber had sent to hunt them down. William Waltz should have had the death shot, or at least a completely debilitating one with little difficulty as the shrapnel bore into the target. But when Waltz had tried to take down the driver, the son of a bitch had tumbled away in a freakishly fast reaction that should not have been possible.

There has to be tech allowing him to do that, he thought between his inhalation and exhalation. His breathing was measured to prevent any lack of oxygen that could result in cramping. If there was tech involved, an electronic shock and EMP burst from a pulse grenade should incapacitate the driver.

He tossed the small baseball-sized object, and he heard the sound of it striking a body. The blue lighting engulfed the area of the dell and the tussocks.

"That should" but the fire opened up. The feeling of a slug brushing against the outer lobe nearly stopped his run. The grenade did not work. *How the hell?* he thought.

Waltz held his fire and moved up and down the gentle slope toward the ocean at a run. Foam licked at his feet at times, but the driver could not possibly mark him for long enough to hit him.

I'll never crack whatever tech-shell this guy's wearing without getting up close and personal, he thought.

The hiding place, the grassy knoll, came up quickly. The driver had shot and missed and reloaded twice and was surprised at the full-on frontal assault in the dark. That it was happening as quickly as it was must have been perplexing to the driver, who must have been winded.

Waltz sprinted for a huge kick at the end of the run and dove and tackled the driver backward onto the long grass. The man was much larger in height and weight than Waltz was and soon had flipped Waltz over and gained control.

The forearms that Waltz held in his hands felt like fossilized muscle. The driver was armored in a smoothly flowing substance, a skintight method that was unknown to him. Guessing that electrical signals had to run through the seamless armor, Waltz let go of one of the arms and pulled an EMP knife, pressed the button in the hilt to activate the white lightning, and stabbed the driver in the shoulder with it.

The mech-armor turned the knife. Waltz had just enough time to look on the broken blade with his mouth open before the driver's fist came down and plastered his nose.

70

TURNED

Sheetrock grunted as the knife escaped him and dove into his shoulder blade. He was already grimacing from the blurring options that cascaded across his sight in the tumbling matrix of rain. Then the armor pushed back on the blade. He felt it. The knife was turned. And it was like magic.

71

BATTLE

"Shit" said Waltz through clenched teeth. Blood dripped into his eyes and mouth. His face throbbed. *What the hell happened to Xera?* he wondered.

But before he could complete that series of thoughts, Xera Finn cracked Sheetrock over the head with the side of her gun. While he fell over, she extended the harpoon into Sheetrock's thigh; she had retrofitted it with an EMP that charged the tip.

He yelled in pain, his suit punctured, and leaped back some ten feet involuntarily. The storm had draggled the grass; in Sheetrock's hurry to move, he shuffled his feet, slipped, and fell in the mud. Xera started after him, but Sheetrock crouched and leaped back again off of all four of his limbs to distance himself further. The electromagnetic pulse had not worked, even though she could see his blood as it trailed along the ground's puddles.

Hopefully that'll at least slow the bugger down, she thought.

"I don't know you" said Sheetrock to her. "But you and William Waltz the fugitive are coming with me... dead on the tip of my drill bit (that's an old miner's joke)... or alive. It's up to you."

From the muddy branches, Waltz could see her back stiffen. She had not expected the threat, but more outright bludgeoning first and reasoning later when they were dead or in custody being tortured. Sheetrock knew this, because it was what he had anticipated too. *Who is this guy?*

"He didn't do anything wrong." Xera flexed and prepared to dodge any bursts that might come after her. Her breath showed in the bitter rain.

"I'm just doing my job" replied Sheetrock.

"So was he" she said. He tilted his head in clear astonishment.

From the mud holes at his feet a slimy hand took Sheetrock's ankle in an iron grip and another came up and thrust his torso backward. His body splayed out and went flying. Waltz landed on top of Sheetrock and managed to get in a few blows before the mech-armor gave its wearer the strength to buck up and hurl the fugitive from his body.

Caught in a desperate battle of unknown consequence, the former space-mining captain let the triangular blade extend over the top of his hand. He turned and bent, ready to kill. Then he screamed in anguish the like of which had no rival.

Xera pushed the harpoon tip in a little deeper and let go of the handle. Sheetrock gurgled and fell forward onto his face in the wet grasses and bent reeds. The harpoon was rooted in the base of Sheetrock's spine and sizzled.

She rose and gently pulled out the tiny tip. There was no sign from the man. Waltz joined her and helped to turn Sheetrock over. The man was at least three hundred pounds without the extra weight of the armor, though Waltz doubted the Mech-suit weighed much at all.

Sheetrock had stopped breathing. He was motionless.

"Jesus, I killed him" said Xera so quietly that Waltz barely caught the words over the rustling echoes of the storm.

"It shouldn't have. A simple EMP delivered to the nervous system should have shut down the electrical signals transmitting from the mech-armor. He should be immobile, inert, but not dead."

"This must be a newer suit than we've ever seen or knew existed. It must be intertwined with his spinal column and his brain somehow. I just short-circuited the very electricity that keeps us alive" she said. "God—"

"Are we still looking for a boat?"

"Yes" Xera said composing herself. "After I get a good look at this guy's Jeep."

72

ELECTRICAL IMPULSES

Thunder crackled on the air, and Fae Yu slipped silently beneath its cover and out into the dunes. She had seen them coming. What was worse: she had watched the beating and the murder from her monitor.

I can't believe it. Those bastards killed him. It's my fault. She mourned. *It's all my fault.*

Resilience grew deep in the corner of her thoughts and slowly pushed its way to the front of the crowd. *I can save him. I can. I have to.*

As Xera and Waltz loudly entered the Jeep and rummaged through its contents, Yu crawled. Slowly, she worked her way from the sand to the watery ground to Sheetrock.

He was not breathing. She wiped the mud from in between her fingers and held him. He was gone. She had found a corpse. Thunder cracked, like a whip close by.

No, she reminded herself. She rummaged in her pack and retrieved a small med-cube. *He needs help. He's not gone.* And she fastened the alligator clips to his motionless chest and with a push of an ominously red button sent the current through Sheetrock. The body rose in response. But he did not wake.

Yu turned the juice to the maximum output on the defibrillator and sent the electricity into his body again. That time Sheetrock sat bolt upright and gasped desperately to restart a breathing process. He spat and sputtered but managed to breathe on his own as coughing abated.

Waltz and Xera heard his awakening. But it did not matter. *Because Frankenstein's monster's alive!* Yu thought. "Now pull yourself together, you ox" she whispered. "They're going to try to kill us if you don't."

Sheetrock wiped the rain from his eyebrows and grabbed Yu's face and kissed her long. Before she knew what was happening their lips separated and she was thrown backward into a nearby hedge. Long shadows crossed and sliced through the wet walls of tumblers.

Yu looked up through the cold bristles of the brush and saw flashes of light. Of the three revolving figures, the tallest was Sheetrock, but he crouched low and she soon lost him. Her chest tightened as tremendous anxiety grasped hold.

In a series of blurry moves, Sheetrock approached the fugitives. He crouched, dove, rolled in a ball, and was on his feet moving with a velocity that the three hundred pound man had never dreamed he would be capable of achieving. Sheetrock flew through the pelting rain and each bullet that struck him only seemed to redirect him, like a pinball in an arcade coin-op from days long gone. Pain could not wipe the resolution from his face.

The zigzagging and boxer dancing could not cause the two shooters to completely miss. But Sheetrock circled in closer and closer to Waltz and Xera all the same. His mech-armor absorbed the shrapnel from the hollow rounds that exploded upon impact with his exoskeleton. And he was able to vary his height enough that he avoided their shooting him in the head.

As a result, he was able to reach them and with one burst of unanticipated speed sent a sweeping roundhouse kick of finality. He knocked both of the scatter pistols from their hands, and they went flying into the underbrush, useless.

Sheetrock did not pause, exactly, but he stepped back a pace to catch his breath, while grasping pieces of bloody metal from places on his ribs and torso where the suit was ejecting the scatter shards. Xera seized the opportunity to recover her stance and unfurl a large butterfly knife and embed it in his shoulder blade.

"I'll cut the spine out of you, if that's what it will take" Xera said through clenched teeth. But there was no EMP.

With the force of the descending knife, Sheetrock sank. The weapon cut into him, but not as deeply as she had intended. He sat back on his haunches and went to the ground, wrenching the knife from Xera's hand.

In a moment of anger, Sheetrock felt his armor lower and stretch on top of his knuckles, and he sent a stiffened fist in a roundhouse to the back of Xera's head. She was thrown to the ground unconscious, but before he could mark her further Sheetrock found a rain of blows upon his face. He held up his arms to block Waltz, but the slim cyber-warrior sidestepped him and sent furious punches to the kidney region when he could not touch the head.

Sheetrock was quick in the mech-armor. Yu watched him move with a fluidity that bent the laws of physics and the human anatomy. But Waltz was fast too and attacked relentlessly with a renewed vigor since his partner was hurt badly and lying face up in a growing puddle. He was erratic and despite the force that Sheetrock put behind his own reinforced blows, Waltz merely bounced off of them and went on hurling himself, carelessly, and sent lots of jabs at the eyes and body of his assailant.

It was a recklessly blind assault. And Waltz nearly dazed Sheetrock enough to knock him off of his feet.

Sensing this, Yu cocked her own gun and prepared to intervene.

But the biotech in a semiautonomous move of self-preservation drew back the material covering Sheetrock's knuckles and put forth a long, sleek triangular blade in its place. Thought flew from his mind, Yu could see it leave his eyes, and all that played out was the commands: MOVE, MOVE, SLICE.

And then she saw the adrenaline-laced Waltz stumble and back away from Sheetrock. His coat was rent in a tremendous fashion, hanging open. Flesh and blood were exposed to the onslaught of the spray. The ocean roared. Waltz fell to his back.

73

TRAPPED

William Waltz backed up, temporarily unsure of himself. He was split open from left shoulder to opposite hip. The freezing wind jabbed at the open wound across his upper torso causing Waltz's legs to wobble.

The pain came in an immense surge as the freezing air and rainwater pelted his chest. Up until that point, nothing registered but Xera going down, hurt. With the sudden feeling of excruciating stabbing pain, however, his rage and concentration was broken. He began to assess the situation as he always had, practically.

The mammoth figure before him was some kind of new Cyber weapon and, possibly, was not even human. The guy shed hollow-point rounds with barely a grimace and moved with a freakish speed for someone who was that bloody big and had been shot to pieces (and tramping on sodden ground too). And then the blade of some hidden katana had come out of nowhere and sliced him up.

Waltz had heard weird tales of mechanized symbiotic armor whispered of in the dark corners of directorate buildings (both Cyber's and other governmental ones). He knew there was truth in such rumors when his own warrior colleagues embedded permanent computer tech directly into their bodies, and half of them did not even try to hide it. The public feared the age of robotics, from the patrolling B.O.N.E.S. and helidrones on every town square, to the glowing artificial eyes of the wealthy who mimicked the once injured cyber-warriors out of some misplaced sense of Cyberian fashion. But technology was pressing forward that way, all too quickly, for good or ill.

A terrible idea surfaced. Waltz had to act on it. A terrible idea could not be ignored. He turned and he ran toward the beach. *I'm going to die face down in the sand*; he chuckled to himself. The rain tore at his wound and he stopped laughing long enough to grimace.

The thick patches of bushes and tussocks slapped Waltz as he strode past. He was sure that Sheetrock would probably shoot him down on the spot, but he felt he had to take the chance and hoped the spouts of rain amidst the winter swamp might hide his back long enough to escape.

It hurt to breathe. *I can at least stall the bastard long enough for Xera to escape.* He turned and twisted – more shots fired – but kept on southwards.

The pace quickened. The hillocks of sand parted and the land declined. Bursts rang out and kicked up sand at his feet.

Then smooth foam licked his ankles. Waltz's heart nearly stopped for the cold. He waited to drag Sheetrock into the collapsing waves. Waltz would let his surfing ability help him to stay afloat in the tumultuous ocean, giving an advantage. *Come on in so I can drown your ass,* thought Waltz.

At the top of the gray dunes, Sheetrock emerged and stood tall.

"Come on! You want me? You can fish me out of here! I bet you never caught a trout this big!" shouted Waltz. He hoped he would not have to go any further into the frigid water to lure Sheetrock out; the forty-degree temperature would seize Waltz up in minutes (after all, he did not have a Mech-suit or so much as a wetsuit but only a three-button wool suit), and he had to drown Sheetrock before the gray world faded away to nothing.

Xera will come to. She'll be able to put me in front of a heater and revive my broken body, thought Waltz. He shook his head and felt the drops streak down his cheeks. *What a pipedream.*

The silhouette of the tall man hunched in the light of the storm. He was intent on staring Waltz down. Sheetrock stooped, lifted a large spear-like object from a pack. There was no sound whatsoever.

Without warning the great net fired into the ocean and enclosed Waltz and a five feet diameter, all around him. A gas-powered spear was pointing out of the sand in front of him and from it the net was pulled in. It coiled itself on the thin pole and retracted and Waltz was swept off his feet and dragged to the bounty hunter's object until his head touched it.

His arms and legs were forced together cruelly and the pressure of the silky Kevlar net was excruciating. He could not move at all. It was truly over.

74

SHOOT

Sand caked his swollen nostrils, and the net tightened. Waltz could barely breathe. Blood dripped from his aching nose and into his mouth. He gasped, his lips twisting against the gridded rope that clawed into his face.

The dark gray seemed to deepen on the shrinking horizon, as Sheetrock approached. Waltz could not move. He could only watch as his adversary grew in his line of sight.

"I'd like to take you in alive, Mr. Waltz. But something tells me that it'd be a huge mistake. Your mind is too keen on escape" said Sheetrock. The regret in his voice was genuine. "This is a job I have to complete, and it's either you or me."

The remains of the long, tattered duster parted and Sheetrock pulled a B9 from a holster hanging loosely from his hips. The *wush* of a wave came in, and it soaked Waltz's body. He shivered uncontrollably with cold and fearful for the bitter end to what he thought to be a meaningless life conducted in service of country, of Cyber, and for nothing else (and thus, wasted).

Sheetrock turned on a dime and fired his pistol into the night behind where he stood. Somehow he had detected an intruder, but despite whatever thermals or other digital interfaces to lock onto the target that he had used, Sheetrock missed. A blast caught his forearm, causing him to drop his gun.

Before Sheetrock could stoop to recover his B9, a female battle cry accompanied three rounds landing into his armored chest. Sheetrock fell back into the shallow water beside Waltz.

But the blows and the ocean only delayed his dominance. As Xera strode up, he was already encircling her position, and in a series of feigning jabs, rolled over into a frontal somersault, kneeled, and dealt a lethal elbow to her midsection. She spat and was rooted to the sand, the air driven from her. Sheetrock took her by the neck.

"No!" cried Waltz.

Sheetrock threw Xera in a heap onto the tightened net where Waltz lay paralyzed. Sheetrock recovered his scatter pistol, sighed, and dusted it off. He slowed with time, reluctant to kill them outright, even for Cyber and country and the almighty dollar.

"Go ahead! Murder us outright, you monster! Your 'fugitive' has done nothing wrong except serve his Cyber masters as they commanded until they felt the need to discard him, because he was too good" said Xera. There was an awkward silence and Sheetrock tilted his head.

"Murder us both. My most recent crime is trying to right the injustice of William's situation. You people ought to be ashamed. But I guess you're just their lackey anyway. Their mechanized enforcer. Their cold-blooded bastard. You have no conscience anymore, do you?" she went on. "You're not even human."

The strange pause seemed to quell the rush of the water about them and the crying wind from the storm. Sheetrock, without looking, fingered sand out of the barrel of the gun. He checked the clip and refastened it in place. But he was stalling, at least for a little while.

"God as my witness... I love you, Xera Finn" whispered Waltz. She ignored him and went on.

"Do it! Come on! Do it! Shoot us! SHOOT!"

75

PATIENCE

Sheetrock raised the hand cannon. He had had enough. The woman had played on his conscience and hurt him.

"I was hoping my magnet would've fried your guts from the inside out. But it didn't. SO SHOOT ALREADY!"

He zoned out. The smash of each falling wave spoke with a unique tone, and he thought back to the Cyber headquarters lobby where he had sat in waiting that very same day.

* * *

The heavy glass doors shook with the weight of a thousand protestors. The sounds of each impassioned citizen pierced the impenetrable walls. And the cry of the young demonstrator, the woman, shook his bones.

Sheetrock was terrified. He might lose his mech-armor, his life, and worse, Yu's life.

The creepy tope walls held a pair of six-foot long posters. The message did not help to ease his mood.

"NO!"

The first said: DON'T WORRY. WE WATCH ALL AND KEEP YOU SAFE. There were six drones of varying sizes photographing people stealing money at a farmer's market in a city square and people assembling bombs on children's school desks.

"No! No!"

The second poster read: YOU COULD NOT HAVE A FRIENDLIER GUARD DOG. This featured a soldier smiling as a B.O.N.E.S. bot pushed his helmet up over his head, while three soldiers looked on laughing delightedly.

"Nooooo" THUD

The baton hit the hollow skull beneath the woman's dreadlocks hard. The guards circled around and took turns beating her, as she curled up in the fetal position whimpering.

THUD

It took every fiber of his being to not rush the B.O.N.E.S. and the soldiers and attempt to put a stop to the merciless beating. He knew the result of such an action. He knew he needed to hide in plain sight, where he sat, until Cyber had agreed to hire him and in so doing offered amnesty for his body within the suit that was their stolen property.

THUD THUD

If she doesn't die quickly, I'm going to lose it, lose everything; 'cause I'll stop this madness, thought Sheetrock. It was still playing in his mind as the protestors burst through the open doors.

* * *

"Do it!" Xera bellowed. The finger grazed the trigger, gingerly rubbed the trigger, back and forth. Waltz winced but could not look away. He may have wanted to close his eyes, but they were wide and looking up at Sheetrock to see death come.

"Coward! Are you having doubts?"

Back and forth.

"DO IT!"

Back and forth. Sheetrock's mind swayed.

Back and forth. If Waltz was wrongly accused of espionage and treason, then it would be another act of murder further bloodying the hands of the Cyber Elite; that called into question a fundamental feeling of nationalism that had always led Sheetrock to be a good citizen, following the laws, and acting honestly, paying his God's forsaken taxes, and helping his fellow Cyber brother and sister when he could. And the Elite, though their identities were unknown to the public, helped guide Congress, the President, and the Supreme Court. But if they were flawed...

Back and forth. The wind whistled with the steady onslaught of rain, but the waves crashed down and onto the shore and then retreated from where they came from. They stood within a circle, a mire. The process repeated.

"Who the hell are you?" Sheetrock blared out. His nerve was shot; his anxiety superseded all else. Everything had somehow shifted and spun off the rails.

"My name is Xera Finn, and I am aiding a fugitive who is innocent of all the charges Cyber has pinned on him."

"I have to do this, Xera Finn."

"William Waltz is being erased. He exposed a hidden Cyber agenda to arm their enemies in hopes that they would murder their own regions with outright genocide. They hope that there will be little left standing when they step on the throats of survivors and rule us all with an iron fist."

The B9 pistol shook in Sheetrock's hand, a hand that had been sure and steady throughout an entire life of physical labor that required it. He was in disbelief.

"The Elite have forgotten their roots. The hackers turned on the governments they served to undo abuse and to undo the backroom deals with corporations and other powerful organizations. The hackers fought to undo the growing tyranny with Cyber."

The left hand came over and doubled over the right. Sheetrock looked through the sight and felt the smooth hardness of the curved trigger mechanism on the inside of his finger.

"Don't you get it? Or did they not brief you on why you were to kill this man? William uncovered a corporate CEO that Cyber used to support foreign governments around the world. Cyber could not act lawfully, so they arranged for some of the wealthiest corporate leaders to profit immensely and attain their own small amount of real power in Cyber Programmers who were assigned to them and unknowingly enslaved to the illegal corporate dealings. When a programmer found out about it, they were killed. It was simple... at least until William came around."

Sheetrock took a deep breath to clear it all from the mind and do what needed to be done.

"NO!" cried Yu running up beside him. He had nearly squeezed on hearing the sound of her voice.

76

A NEW TURN

“Yu?” Sheetrock started. He pulled the gun up and then pistol-whipped Waltz with it.

“Yu? Fae Yu?”queried Xera. Waltz saw double.

“Fae!” He looked from side to side dumbfounded.

“DON’T HURT HIM!” screamed Yu. She threw herself at Sheetrock’s arm holding the gun.

“You know each other?” he said. “It doesn’t matter. I still have to do this. He’s too dangerous to try and take in alive.”

“He’s not the enemy. Not if Xera’s with him.”

“Cyber’s turned on him, as they have their own people” said Xera. “This man’s done nothing wrong except get recruited by Cyber when he was a toddler after his parents died.”

“Xera, I had no idea it was you until I heard the shouting” said Yu. She paused and leaned on her knees to slow her breathing from the run across the dunes.

“Hon, this is a good friend of mine” she said. “One of the few I have and I’m sorry you’ve never met her before. But... you see... we’re often together when you’re out in space for months at a time. But Xera’s often out of town too. She was the one who acquired the intelligence and the ID lenses of General Rancor that were integral in getting me into Cyber’s R&D level where your armor was kept. Put the gun down.”

"I'm supposed to just let him go?" Sheetrock asked softly.

"Yes, hon. Xera is not lying."

"What's this man's real name, Xera? Did you find that out?"

"It's William Sheetreich. He has one living relative, an uncle named Benjamin."

"Oh hell" Sheetrock replied and lowered the B9.

77

FINALITY

The ten-foot tall iron gates to Joshua Franciscus's cattle farm opened outward with a squeal. Xera Finn typed in another alarm code on her phone's screen and the corroded gates clanged behind their advancing Mini and shut out the outside world.

Franciscus hid himself in the middle of the rural country. The Chimacum valley rested in Washington's Olympic Peninsula, about four miles from the Pacific Ocean. The area had many new-gen farms dating back to the early twenty-first century. And it was the rainiest place in the region formerly known as the continental United States; the result, Waltz saw, was fields of thick marsh grasses being hungrily chewed up by dozens of cows. This was the rich turf of farm country.

Waltz held the back of his head and winced. The stitches were still bothering him and the itch was pure madness. The fever that had nearly roasted him alive for two days had abated with antibiotics that Xera had insisted he take.

"Are you sure these stitches are sterile, Xera?" he asked feigning concern.

"Don't you dare start with me" she said, and they turned up a muddy driveway where lines of woods drew up on either side and hid the cows from their view. She did flash him a smile as she said it at least. *She must feel bad for my scalped ass,* thought Waltz.

At the end of the wooded lane was an enormous farmhouse that stood three stories tall. The outside looked old, but well maintained and freshly painted. A long wooden porch stretched the width of the maroon building and on it sat half a dozen sentries on swinging benches hanging from chains in the roof.

"This is just a front" said Xera. "Joshua's home stretches back much further than the naked eye can tell in the freakin' rain; it's an illusion. And my guess is he's got a small city buried half a mile underground. That's where his hospital and his drug processing facilities stand guarded by his own private army barracks.

"Geez, are you serious?" asked Waltz. She did not answer.

The car circled around a small fountain where a chubby cupid pissed water from a stone phallus. She decided to take that as a sign and park where Cupid was pointing, on the right side of the lane's end. For the time being she wanted to face the guards straight off.

"Try to behave, please. I want to get on this guy's good side before he owns my ass."

"I do not believe in behaving, William. It's part of why I do what I do" she replied. "And it's why Joshua and I do not get on so well. Life's a bitch, but rules are worse."

They approached the great stair leading up to the porch, and six strapping young men, in overalls (for pulling off the full farmer effect), rose and unholstered six old-fashioned .357 magnum revolvers. *Place appears to be up on the times,* thought Waltz, as he was handed a candle lantern and led inside, at least for backwoods cousin kissing (if the stereotypes held any water).

"Right this way please, Ms. Finn. Mr. Joshua's been expectin' you folks for some time now" said the leader. For such a tall and robust figure, he had a high-octave voice that seemed a bit out of place amidst the other hard-nosed farmhands.

With a wave they were escorted into an old-fashioned southern manor court with two enormous staircases bordering the room. Hustling down the set on the right was a short, dumpy man looking about twenty.

"Ms. Finn and our new distinguished guest, my name is Manny. Please allow me to welcome you to the Franciscan Manor" he said.

Manny met them at the foot of the stairs and shook each of their hands limply, as though he were holding a dead fish up to look at in the light. His butler attire was so tight that it might tear at any sudden movement required of him.

"Please follow me to the barn for our preliminary examination of your – ah – gentleman, Ms. Finn" he said with a smile and a measuring look at Waltz.

"Yes, of course" she said. But Waltz could tell that this had caught her off guard.

After many twists and turns through numerous corridors they found themselves back out in the rain and on their way to a colossal barn up ahead. Manny led them up the wet path and three of the guards followed closely behind. *What the hell are we going to a barn for?* he thought.

The cracked and worn slats separated into two doors. The mouth was dark. They stepped into the dimness of the barn.

It was extremely hot and the air felt moist. An enlarged B.O.N.E.S. model dragged a heavy black bag to a roaring furnace and with a flick of its spring-loaded tail threw the bag into the flames and shut the grate with a metallic paw. It grew brighter and wiry shadows danced around the orange light.

"You can wait outside with the guards, Manny" said a voice from behind them. A blinding florescent light beamed out of crevices in between the great iron piping that grew from the furnace and climb up into the third story loft.

Waltz turned and saw a squat shaped man who was only a fraction taller than Manny, who turned and left abruptly. Their portly host held a small remote pointed toward the lights, which dimmed considerably.

"There we are. I wanted you to see me, but at the same time I don't like anyone to know that I have electricity anywhere, because they'd wonder where the power came from and why I never set up a utility account."

"Mr. Waltz is it? I'm Joshua Franciscus, and this is my barn, my land."

"We figured as much, Joshua. Why are we in here exactly?" asked Xera suspiciously.

There was a wry smile that came to the pasty face and the thin pedophile mustache twitched in his round head. He scratched a head of thin balding wisps of hair and held out a hand with a half-bow quite dramatically.

"Look around you."

The entire barn was filled with iron and copper piping (from widths of less than an inch to diameters that were a foot across), hand valves, and glass gauges. Electric motors whined on great cast pumps churning massive amounts of water. Wisps of steam spit from various valves. The facility could power a small city or town.

"There are solar panels hidden in every place that might catch a rare ray of sunshine, but out here that's not enough to power my needs" said Joshua. "This steam-powered generator room can. It's run on burning trash. I seem to have no end of the garbage coming out of my ears. So I burn it, and there's heat and steam and the world turn's round without being any wiser to the fact." He laughed maniacally and was disturbingly happy showing off his own cleverness.

"I do not meet in my conference room anymore because of the trouble I've had cleaning up the mess left by the less interesting... interviewees. We negotiate here now, Xera. The reason being: if your boy and I do not come to an agreement, then you can both further my energy needs for as long as it takes to burn your bodies to ash. This barn is a clean place."

"That's not necessary. Look" she started.

"Oh really? He's a fuckin' cyber-warrior! And you brought him here? God knows why after all I've done to avoid Big Brother Cyber's eye. I mean, what the fuck were you thinking?"

"He's in a position of power and can offer you more access than you've ever had to the Cyber facilities, to all of their tools, their files."

"I hope he can also give one hell of a blowjob, because otherwise—" said Joshua.

"Hey asshole, I'm not blowin' anybody. You got it?" said Waltz. "Let's not talk like that in front of the lady, okay? I've got a good offer: how would you like to feed your own fire... want to bet we could fit your pudgy ass in there?"

"Sparky" said Joshua softly. The robotic dog bounded to him and sat at his feet; sitting down the B.O.N.E.S. was as tall as Joshua was standing up.

"Joshua, you ever wonder what the Cyber government's got on you?" asked Xera calmly.

"They don't have anything on me. I'd be in custody if they did" he replied.

“Unless they had everything, the who, what, why, and, when, except the where. Your present whereabouts are unknown. But you’re still on all of the Wanted posters. You’ve done a heck of a job concealing yourself and your entire operation beneath this rural center, but if your file remains open they will find you and shut down your—”she paused and spoke with disdain, “private surgical and drug industries. And then you won’t be able to work for money, sex, and an unending high.”

“You stupid bitch!” He lashed out and backhanded Xera across the jaw. She fell to the floor.

“The last person that insulted me is still alive, you know. I visit them every day in the test subject center; their brain is mush and they’ll never get to walk or extend their arms because of permanent restraints, but you can learn a hundred times more about a drug’s effectiveness and side effects from a human test subject than you can from any animal or computer simulation. Shall I introduce”

“No!” interrupted Waltz. He leaped over Xera and engaged the B.O.N.E.S. The oversized bot took a direct approach that the trained agent anticipated. As the metal dog bounded forward, Waltz dove directly in between the creature’s legs. As its head dropped to tear out his throat, Waltz reached his hand deep into the pivoting neck and pulled from it a thick cable with a snap. B.O.N.E.S. dropped to the floor. Then Waltz dusted himself off and punched Joshua across the mouth.

“Mother fucker! Do you think that’ll make me do what you want?”

“No, but I hope you’ll think twice before striking a lady again.”

“He works for Cyber” said Xera emphatically.

"And made a most useful pageboy I expect" said Joshua. He reached out and slapped Waltz's ass. "Eh?" He laughed and this time the sound was far more high-pitched and eerie against the sound of thunder and rainfall.

"I was a cyber-warrior and pegged to become one of the Elite. I can infiltrate their entire order if"

"You sucked all of their winky-dinks and then their sons!" cried Joshua with glee. There was no way the surgeon was anything approaching sobriety.

"If I have a new face" said Waltz finishing his own sentence quietly. Saying it made the thought of it being done to him, permanently, somehow sharper and cut deeper.

"A new face, D.N.A. pattern, and cellular reconstruction" said Joshua. "Yes, that would be enough to fool them, provided you have enough knowledge and resources to get past all of the Cyber security features that are in place. And I guarantee they'll add new ones now that you're a dead man in their eyes."

78

REMOTE CONTROL

The move was subtle. Joshua Franciscus rubbed his reddening jaw; the color stood out in stark contrast to his pale, corpse-like skin tone. And then he reached for his remote.

Xera did not miss anything. Her reaction was visible as a slight tightening of her stance. Waltz picked up on it immediately.

From the roof beams of the barn came a fleet of Firefly helidrones. The Fireflies dropped quickly and silently. Their priming electrical tasers gave each a supernatural glow, or halo. Three-dozen orbs of bluish-white light descended upon their targets.

The massive furnace's fire popped and hissed, as if to recognize the oncoming assault. Joshua sat himself on the ground and began to slowly scoot on his butt away from Xera and Waltz. He knew the Fireflies were deadly and would not stop firing until the two interlopers were no longer moving. And that included breathing, which they had been programmed to look for in their victims' chests rising and falling. Joshua did not want to get caught in their way.

But as the bobbing helidrones flew down, Xera dove to the left and Waltz to the right. The confused bots split up. Xera threw a baseball-sized EMP into the air and with a blast of lightning the entire Firefly fleet crashed to the floor, stunned. Waltz produced one of the magnets she had given him and walked over each twitching drone and pressed the magnet to it causing small puffs of smoke and the stillness of finality.

He approached Joshua. Waltz was unable to hide the expression of smugness from in between his narrow cheekbones. Xera joined him frowning. Her brow was wrinkled in concern. *Why was she so worried?* Waltz wondered.

"Do you know what your provocation just cost me, you little shit?" asked Joshua. His eyes, covered in swollen capillaries, narrowed. The cost and the smile hurt the negotiations badly, and Waltz felt his scrotum shrink.

"You can see that he means business, Franciscus. And he's too thickheaded to hear you say, 'no.' What the hell do you want from us to make the deal?" asked Xera.

"It's simple. Only complete compliance will seal our agreement. Anything less and I'll upload his mug and his new DNA information all over the web to make sure this meeting never occurred. He'll be swallowed up instantaneously. I won't even have to lift a finger."

"What are the terms?" she asked impatiently while Waltz looked on at the real bargaining as an outsider. Franciscus would not even treat with him, or even look at him anymore. Preliminary negotiations had ended and he was altogether left out of the final part of the process.

"The terms: infiltrate Cyber's entire network and find out what they have on me; if their files are as thorough as you imply, I'll want them erased, all traces except for the Elite themselves. This should warn them against pursuing me any further and keep you alive. Because if you cracked their ranks, you would not survive long enough to tell me about it."

"We can do that."

"I'm not finished" said Joshua rudely.

"Go on" she said impassively. Waltz was amazed at how cool she kept – how she swallowed up the anger that she had to feel coursing through her cells. He could not have done it.

"If I'm to do this, I need a bigger investment. It will require the long con. I want to see him not only infiltrate the cyber-warrior's ranks but also to make them fill the seat he left behind when 'William Waltz' disappeared."

"He'll be my agent. He'll report everything to me. A cyber-warrior of my own, approved by the Cyber echelon, is all it will take to seal the deal."

"You want him to serve you as a member of Cyber for life?" asked Xera unbelievingly.

"Yes. A life of servitude is better than death. Did you get all of that, Manny?" asked Joshua to the stenographer above him. A sound buzzed from an intercom in the barn.

"Yes, boss."

"Good. Write up the contract with those exact terms."

Waltz felt dizzy. The ground swelled beneath his feet and the room grew steadily darker until he knew no more.

"Well... I'm sorry but that's not going to fly. I can't possibly agree to"

Xera cut him off before he could finish.

79

BOUNTY

"Where are the bodies?"

"I don't have a body."

"What do you mean you don't have a body?" asked Ro quietly. The small square room was lined with filing cabinets that rose to the ceiling. Ro licked pink lips.

Sheetrock shook his head.

"The girl abandoned Waltz and drove on without him, scared for her own skin" said Fae Yu. Ro's fury was palpable. "We're waiting for leads from the local authorities and the satellite imagery, but she may have hitched a ride to Canada by now for all we know."

"He's allowed the murderous traitor to live on, unscathed" whispered Jasmine. Her pale cheeks reddened considerably and one of her eyes clouded over black and metallic.

"Hardly 'unscathed'" said Yu.

Sheetrock tossed a large patch of scalp and hair onto the floor between the two cyber-warriors' feet. He wiped his big hand on the outside pocket of his new black trench coat.

"I don't allow traitors to live" he said with a glower for the cyber-warriors' interrogation. "We fought on the water. And I wasn't drowning for your sake." His voice was flat and gruff.

The agents did not seem to hear him; they stared at the clump of hair and blood and skin. Ro looked ready to be sick. It was evidence. Thunder clapped loudly outside the Manhattan building.

"Okay. Can somebody please get this over to analysis? I want this confirmed as William Waltz's DNA before Benjamin Sheetrock and Fae Yu leave here today. And bring a mop!" said Jasmine Ribaldi.

She got up from the stainless steel table and knocked on the heavy door. The thud produced a one-eyed teenage boy with a small rubber box. Jasmine left the room.

"I apologize" said Ro. "That was very unprofessional of her."

"It's quite alright" said Yu. "You're our bosses.

"Once the DNA is verified" said Ro, "go and help the scientists figure out why it is Sheetrock survived the armor binding process and all of their human test subjects do not. One more thing."

"The scalp is William's then?"

"It is" said Sheetrock grimly. He crinkled his face and the beard he had begun to grow twitched a little near one of his eyes. Ro nodded and left the room.

"I guess that's a no" said Yu. "What a bitch."

80

213 DAYS LATER

"You know we could very easily be shot and killed tonight" said Fae Yu. She clicked off the living room light and turned on a small lamp by the door. The wind whistled in the eave and shook their windows.

"I know. We're doing this to change things for the better. There's no going back. Willy can't go back" said Sheetrock.

"I know. It's just—"

"Shush now, little lady. The hour's not far off. Change often requires sacrifice. But I haven't gone into the asteroid mines, breathed in their cancer, and had you save me so that we'd get hurt on payday. We do this and life gets easier from here on out. We'll be fine, Fae."

It was more than she had ever heard him say at one time. Normally, once Yu got going, she would dominate each conversation. He spoke in short sentences, in clumps of two or three words at a time tops. Regardless of his confident, comforting words, Yu drew close to him. She pressed her mouth up and into his. The hour was not far off. But there was time enough. Their lips closed on one another's.

The Mech-suit became translucent and thin. Yu tore at Sheetrock's clothes and when they were in a heap on the hardwood floor she leaped atop him with her legs about his waist. Wherever she touched, the armor folded away so that her skin met his. He could never detach from the suit, but reeled itself back and rolled up to his spine and allowed him, and her, access to his softer human body.

He yelped in surprise as Yu attacked him. She bit Sheetrock's collarbone and clawed at his chest hair. She screamed and scratched at the line bordering seething pain and incomparable pleasure.

He gently lifted her and threw her onto the couch, back down. The lightning brightened the room for an instant. And their bodies, slick with sweat in each other's arms, merged and rocked back and forth.

81

THE PLATTER

"Your information has been very useful, but it's not what we agreed" said Joshua Franciscus. The glow of his jack-o-lantern-like face gleamed in its short three-dimensional projection emanating from Waltz's clear glass phone; he rued the day Xera had given it to him. Joshua did not let up on him for an hour, let alone a day. Providing Cyber intel had become something more than a full-time gig.

"I'm working every avenue I have. You can't expect me to just waltz in there and reclaim my spot as a cyber-warrior among the brethren. It often takes years" said William. He sat on his couch in a converted garage studio apartment in New York. The hilly Miller Place wood provided great privacy outside his doors.

"Ha! You said 'waltz'!" said Joshua. "Well keep this in mind: if you're not blowin' me or a warrior you have a year before the nanobots' acid retainers I embedded in that pretty new face of yours starts to liquefy your head around you."

"I got it, okay? I have a plan. Just take what I give you for now and I'll have a ton that I'll be sharing once I'm officially in Cyber again. I—"

"Shut up! I don't want excuses, you backwoods Long Island Jabroni. I'm going to feast on your juicy ass on a platter for breakfast."

"Silver" interrupted Waltz.

"What?"

"Silver platter."

"What the fuck are you talkin' about?"

"Never mind."

"You think you're smart, but you're not smarter than me! You'll never find the microscopic bits of poison touring your head, and if I do not treat you by the first, you're going to suffer a long and painful rotting. And speaking of your ass, I'm going to"

"I'll get into Cyber, Joshua."

"That's right, you will. And you got less than two months to satisfy me thoroughly before I even consider giving you another treatment. I'm going on a vacation to Thailand, and when I come back from the sex capital, you'd better impress the fuck out of me, William. You ever see what Medusa looked like in the movie"

Waltz hung up the phone and nearly threw the block of it into the ground in anger.

The island hideaway would not keep Joshua out. If Waltz was caught fooling anyone with his new identity, the place would not hold off Cyber from finding him for long either. He sat back and breathed out heavily. *I need a better plan,* he thought morosely.

"Fuck me."

82

REPLACEMENT

"We still have yet to replace the traitor, William Waltz" said Keegan Agnetti. "Our number is one short, at twenty-two, and we are vulnerable."

"Over the past month I came up with a method we might try: have we informed his family? Maybe he had a child that would be capable of being groomed for the position. He held it for a long time and from a very young age, after all."

Agnetti slipped his index finger behind his eye patch and into his socket to itch there. He did it whenever a meeting ran long. The circle of Cyber looked away from him in disgust.

"He has no family. A sister was lost to a drone attack in the Mediterranean three years ago. Their parents died when they were toddlers, trampled as a raving mob of protestors fled Liberty Square fearing a biological agent had been unleashed in the area. No one else remains. We have to look outside the ranks, since none of us have produced a child that has grown near to the age of ten yet" said Ro somberly.

The mood was serious bordering ominous. It was one of the responsibilities of the cyber-warrior to maintain a level of chastity with everyone outside the Round Room so that they would copulate amongst themselves and keep the hope for exceptional Cyber talent and potential future Cyber Elite leaders alive. And it was their vow to make Cyber families and find the select of their children to be initiated into the cyber-warrior ranks. Waltz had not adhered to this as strictly as they had wanted. And now they had his position to fill, and no one liked to talk of trusting an outsider with their identities.

"William Waltz has been erased. It's true. Let's cease talk of him. We need a new lead" said Ro.

"Who put your tits and balls in charge?" asked Connor sarcastically.

A loud clash of egotistical voices filled the room. The rabble amidst the round garden of desks and computers had become harsher than was warranted for a working environment. It was supposed to be a haven from the distractions of the outside world and an altar for the digital Cyber brethren to expand their family, their resources, their skills, and their governing abilities.

Ro rose and strode to the curvilinear walls and walked around with a hand outstretched, skimming the foam surface. It was a walk resembling a model on a runway. Slowly Ro unfastened the black suit jacket and slung it over an arm.

In place of Ro's normal gabardine slacks were women's tight black pants. Regardless of Ro's age (of somewhere near forty), facial features, wild hair, or transgenderness in general, the hips that gave way to the small, round buttocks was very feminine to all in that room. The arguments continued to fly, but many of the eyes followed the cyber-warrior circling the room with a blood-rattling hunger. And with that knowledge and satisfaction, Ro left the Round Room.

83

RO

The Cyber café was open all hours and saw constant activity. All employees were encouraged to stay on as long as it took them to conclude their work, which was why bunking quarters and never-ending food and coffee services were available to the government workers at no cost. Ro sipped a coffee from a tall table that was little bigger than a stool and had no chair.

Racquel, Agnetti, Elizabeth, Harrelson, Connor, and Geva emerged from a hallway and nearly fell over one another in their simultaneous open-mouthed gawking. Ro was leaning, with elbows on the table, standing, but bent slightly back toward them. The tight black pants seemed to shimmer in the dimly lit café.

They noticed that Ro's hair had been shaved along the sides to allow for a short, freely flowing mane, not unlike a mohawk but different. There was an edge there, like always, but a much more feminine feel too.

Geva, who in her extremely experienced twenty-five years was really only interested in men, regardless of the circumstance, could not help but stare down the white dress shirt to the two perfect ass cheeks wiggling up and down (and put on display with the painted-on pants), as a soul singer dominated the coffee house's speakers. She felt a flutter in her chest and a carnal desire tear through her normally perfunctory sexual appetite.

Geva saw that her usual sexual partner, Bud Harrelson, had a bulge in his jeans and had begun to lead their crowd over to Ro's tiny table in the shadowy corner of the Cyber building's café. Jealousy ripped at propriety and stung and at the same time deepened the exotic thoughts and feelings. She grasped his bicep, but Harrelson continued and marched right up to Ro.

Despite the years of outspoken rebuke of a transgender achieving anything, let alone while in their ultra-exclusive ranks, Ro greeted her outspoken colleagues with a beautiful, perfect smile. Each of the would-be suitors began to fight for the opportunity to say something to Ro and grab more attention and after thirty seconds a thin hand was raised up to silence everyone.

"Let's cut through it" said Ro quietly. "I'm horny as fuck and you are too, or you would not have all come over here grinning like you are now."

Their faces fell. Red ripened in all of their cheeks and anger started to twist their expressions. Geva felt she would die from embarrassment; to be rebuked and sent away by a transgender was more than she could fathom, in terms of social society.

"Do not misunderstand me. I am very glad that you all came over here to join me" said Ro with another golden smile. "And that's what I'm hoping we can all do now; join... and fuck."

Comprehension, relief, and renewed sexual throbbing swelled in them.

"All of us?" whispered Geva.

"Yes. Do not worry, ladies" said Ro taking Racquel and Geva's hands. "I am aware of your appetites. And since we all need to help try and build more little cyber-warriors in our family I suggest you come back to my studio where three of my friends – three up and coming Cyber agents – would be happy to help satisfy us all. They are one man and two women, and you know two of them: Ben Sheetrock and Fae Yu. Together we can all have experiences worth living for."

"But that's forbidden" said Keegan Agnetti harshly.

"Sweet, sexy, Keegan, who do you think came up with that rule? That's right, I did" said Ro. He looked abashed. "We need to replace one of our own quickly and more importantly, ensure our future survival. I have already been with these three fertile souls on many an occasion and can ensure you complete discretion. We can make a habit of this. And besides, my mystery lady is as hot as a pistol."

The room had disappeared from view. Visions played on each of their eyes. There was only the dully lit round table and the warriors and Ro who sipped a coffee and licked it off two full lips slowly. The mug emptied.

"That's it for me, I'm afraid" said Ro. "I guess have a boring, old—"Ro stopped and whispered, "foursome to attend."

Without another word Ro turned and started away from them. Geva looked down at Harrelson who was still breathing heavy and took a deep breath. *I'm not going to give them a chance to eat this up*, she thought. *They have to get this out of their system right now.*

Geva shouldered her satchel, flung her long, blonde hair over one shoulder, and stomped loudly (in seven-inch heels) after Ro. Geva reached Ro and put an arm through and held onto the crook of Ro's elbow. Within seconds their group hurried beside them. Before they knew it they were whisked away from the shelter of the building and out into the storm.

84

HOT PIECE

"Come on in, the door's open!" said Sheetrock. "We got started without you." The door rattled as it opened. Ro held it open for the group to quickly pass inside.

They made their way, wiping their feet on the large entrance mats, into the cavernous high-ceilinged apartment and stopped and looked at a very tall man in boxer shorts. Sheetrock held a naked woman in his great arms and was lying on a mattress in the middle of the studio floor. She played with his beard with a thin forefinger.

"Comrades" said Ro holding the door open, "I'd like to introduce you to—"

"Benjamin Sheetrock and Fae Yu" said Keegan Agnetti cutting Ro off rudely.

"But he's so old!" cried Geva. The thought of being with a forty-something year old did not seem to appeal to her.

"Where's this other 'hot piece of ass?'" asked Agnetti hungrily.

"Right here, mother fucker" said Xera as she came into the studio. She held aloft a heavy slab of magnet and looked both gorgeous in the tight black jumpsuit that accentuated her hourglass shape and terrible in her wrath.

Elizabeth screamed. Racquel, Harrelson, Connor, and Geva's robotic eyes smoked and, with a high-pitched squeal, burst asunder in their skulls. Tiny tongues of fire emitted from their sockets before their bodies fell to the floor instantaneously dead.

Agnetti dove at Xera and knocked her aside. He had just reached the doorway when Sheetrock shot him down with a gun that had been hidden under his pillow. Elizabeth had both of her eyes and no robotics, but she had yelled in horror as her lovers smoked and crumpled around her. The delay was fatal.

When Elizabeth finally stood her ground and unloaded her automatic Sonic 2's clip at the bed where the naked people had somehow conducted their assassinations, it was too late. She missed them utterly. The second she waited to aim and pull, while crying out, allowed Sheetrock and Yu just enough time to roll away before the rounds could find them. They repositioned themselves.

Xera recovered, ran, and smashed the heavy magnet onto the back of Elizabeth's head. Ro emerged and took the magnet. Another blow and another was put in for good measure, and then the cyber-warriors that had been lured there were dead.

Sheetrock and Yu dressed quickly. The gasoline was poured onto the floor. They left the bodies where they lay in a twisted heap of sexual frustration.

Ro let a vague smile crease lips before spitting on the stack of bodies. Xera was on her way out of the house before anyone could place her near the scene. With a nod to the cyborg, Sheetrock, and his lover, Ro left quietly. Before tossing the match and shutting the door to the pyre, Sheetrock got a last word in with the dead cyber-warrior that had insulted him.

"Old! Nice to meet you too" he said scratching at his new beard growth and closing his heavy coat with a shake of his head.

85

THE LAB

The lab was unnaturally bright, white, and quiet. Joshua had built an underground fortress for that very reason. He shut out the rain, the sun, and the federal authorities. He could not have felt further than being a part or a citizen of Cyber the country, Cyber the coalition, and Cyber U.S.A. He was his own country, where he could be high all the time without repercussions.

That was why he had built his own lab. It was self-sustaining, in every way, except that the computers worked on closed servers that framed their search engine functionality and data streaming in a stringently censored feed; it did have as much access to the scientific tools as a conventional lab would, but it was more restricted than Cyber's own secured system in their Manhattan headquarters and it tracked each users' data just as good as Cyber, if not better; he had had help from the cyber programmers at Wangluo. Unlike many modern facilities, his was not fully automated – Joshua had his hand in every aspect of it so that each and every scientist under his employment could not yield any level of control over his.

Joshua rarely slept. He kept a tight watch on and micromanaged all of the many different creations that were cooked up daily. He was obsessed and insisted on staying involved in every level of development and deployment and manufacturing. His egotism made him a rampant control freak in the pharmaceutical, biological, and illicit drug trades, and his shipping company reached every stretch of the globe, regardless of regional regulation. He had opened all of the doors himself and, in his mind, relied on no one. He was a one-man sociopathic genius and a deadly army.

The beakers and flasks took up an entire fifty-yard long steel workbench that never ceased to impress him (even though he had built it himself). A couple of naked women in biohazard masks and smocks stirred liquid elements and heated various chemicals. The bitches could not be trusted around the drugs, so he kept them naked and constantly under his eye, which he rather enjoyed; he had hired them with their asses in mind.

There was not a sound on the factory floor. The place was spotless, just as he liked, and the drugs flowed. The product testing kept the quality and him high all the long day and all the long night. Joshua loved life.

86

TARGETING AN END

Nerve was called for. Even for William Waltz, who had gone through a lot in his young life, it took as much balls as he could muster to break into the compound and access Joshua Franciscus's barn. The wet, foggy night helped him; a mountain bike, Xera's drawn map that he had memorized, and night vision goggles did too. If he failed, then Xera and everyone else he had ever known or associated with would suffer greatly at the hands of the mad surgeon. And that would all be on him, because he selfishly made the deal with the devil in order to not face his own death or attempt to run and hide from the country.

Waltz cracked the door and stepped forward initiating the B.O.N.E.S. It was altogether foolish. Sweat launched itself from the pores in his lower back and forehead, and his palms seemed to flood with wetness. The heavy steps of the robot quickened, but, as luck would have it, the B.O.N.E.S. was on the far side of the barn casting a shadow on the wall that was ten feet high.

The black rain melted into the light of the barn's forge, as he entered further, shut the door, and took the steel pole he had trudged across his handle bars and buried it into the wooden floor. As the bot leaped at him, Waltz turned away and moved the six-foot long spear toward the attacker. The B.O.N.E.S. watched, helplessly, as it landed onto the pole instead of the target. The bot impaled itself; while Waltz stood back and held the spike in place, sparks and fire belched from the thrashing body that soon after found death.

Waltz took another step forward and heard a hum above him. In a moment the backpack was slung off of his shoulder and a laptop and connection cable were produced. They slipped in his hands but he managed to work. Sweat dripped from his eyebrows. Within another ten seconds, he had inserted the line into the bot's carcass. He fidgeted nervously, not daring to move, or look up, as a pinwheel spun round and round on the screen.

The hum grew closer... and... *hummmm...* he was in. The computer screen flashed with life, and a small hologram stretched in front of his face. With a swirl of the hand and a series of clicks the screen blinked in recognition, and the entire fleet of drones descended around him and then landed, peacefully, on the floor.

87

HACKED

A slight *hummmmmm* sounded. The air behind Joshua trembled.

"What the?— "

A blue glow dropped in front of his face. He jumped in fright. No one should have been able to get near him down there. Audio white noise played from the speaker that was duct-taped to the circular drone's belly.

"How's that possible?"

"I worked as a spy for Cyber" said Waltz. "You might think your computers are locked down, but you seem to have forgotten who I used to be and what I used to do. What do you think a cyber-warrior is anyway? Do you think it was hard to hack your security's little air force?" asked Waltz with scorn.

The bolt struck Joshua in the chest and sent excruciating pain through his torso that spread out to the tips of his fingers and toes. Such totalic agony was wholly unknown to him.

"Fuck you!" he said.

"No you won't" said the loud voice of Waltz. "And just so you know: that little guy I sent down to you... let's call 'em Hulk... Hulk won't stop until you're dead... and I am free."

"STOP!" squealed Joshua. He swung clenched fists into the air, but his feeble attempts fell far short of the bobbing drone. His t-shirt burned. "STOPPPPPP!"

"This whole place will blow up" he gasped, "and gas everyone with Ebola for twenty miles!"

"What did you say?" asked Waltz.

"I have to type in the failsafe code every hour or else you're gone, I'm gone, everyone's gone. Stop doing this to me, you fuck!"

"I'm listening. Talk fast."

"Wangluo burrowed out the whole region for me. There are ventilation ducts running for a mile and a half radius around here. All around us, you'll burn and boil your own putrefied organs!" cried Joshua. The electrocution ceased.

"Explain to me why you'd unleash Ebola on your own neighbors and betray your countrymen for Wangluo" said Waltz.

"Because I read *"The Hot Zone"* and became inspired!" said Joshua with a mad bulge to his bloodshot eyes. Waltz felt sick to his stomach. The guy was joking about the deadliest virus on earth being used for mass murder. *Can the Cyber protocol even make it on time?*

But he was resolved to go forward. *Risks were meant to be taken. Measured, not shaken, not stirred... just taken,* Waltz thought grimly. *God, I hope he doesn't do it. He has a choice.*

"If I can't watch 'em die of old age, then you can die watching 'em suffer cellular liquefaction" said Joshua. The drone steadied to a hover and began to shoot him again.

"You sick bastard" said Waltz incredulously. The drone ceased. "Why?"

There was a sound of typing. Keys clacked hard for a minute, while Joshua writhed on the floor and tried to pull it together. The helidrone floated in front of him with its blue taser primed and aimed.

"I grew the Ebola, they provided the dispersal tech. It was an even trade. We felt Cyber needed to be crippled, and I'd just relocate to better facilities. So go ahead... kill me... and you'll watch the second coming of the plague you fucking fascist pig."

HUMMMMMMMM

Smoke rose to Joshua's nostrils as the bot sent thousand-plus volts of electricity into his gluttonous body again.

"DIE PIG!"

"You are a psychopath" said Waltz. The air cracked with thunder.

What Joshua did not realize was that the drone recording his admittance and the threat to unleash the custom-grown Ebola virus strain went not only to the government's communications system and their monitors, but the live feed carried through to the Cyber President's TV in the White House and all of the Cyber levels of personnel up to the cyber-warriors (who would hear about it soon enough once their government building was abuzz and then forward it on to get the attention of the Cyber Elite).

Within seconds the important decision makers in the Cyber government were onto the feed and waiting for approval of protocol by the Elite. Within a couple of minutes, the order had been made – to not take any chances based on the threat – and thermite-plasma missiles fired from the nearest submarine (at an undisclosed location) to chemically eradicate the Ebola virus and the entire Joshua farm with concentrated ultra-high–temperature explosions. The bone white cylinders were disbursed from a submarine not far from Vancouver.

* * *

A small remote detonator appeared in Joshua's pasty white palm. Cloudiness spread across his dark eyes. The electrocution did not cease. And Joshua, to his dying torturous breath, did not understand why. He pressed the button.

"Remember this's your fault" said Joshua writhing in his last agonizing moments. "You gave me no choice. Their pain and suffering, the west fuckin' coast's, their blood's on your hands."

88

THE COST

Feeling a guilt that would never cease to haunt his dreams in wake or in sleep, Waltz reluctantly took credit for hacking and alerting Cyber to Joshua's whereabouts and his stockpile of the Ebola virus. He played the card, and Joshua detonated the facility. But Waltz played the aces while he had them. Doing this, Waltz secured an initiation with his former brethren; he could attempt to rejoin the cyber-warriors under the guise of his new person, with a new untraceable identity. It would perplex them, his anonymity, and he hoped it would be enough of a tip-off to his skills and resources to make them want to employ him at all costs. The future held civilization-shattering events, surely, and the time for their greatest need approached.

The rocket left a trail of curly smoke in its wake, as it came on... tearing through the sheets of rain... south and east. Waltz looked up and bit his lip and clicked away on the machine, seeing the weapon in his mind's eye. He could hear the roaring in his ears. He knew that time was nearly lost.

Waltz finished the business with Joshua Franciscus as best he could. He closed out the hologram and grimaced in the reflection of the screen with a face he did not recognize as his own and closed the laptop. He pinched the narrower, more angled cheeks and shook his head in disbelief. Physically, at least, he was a new person. And it was too late to go back and try and undo what had been done.

He looked over his shoulder half expecting to see the glow of a nuclear blast engulf the windows, the rain, and the horizon. The mushroom cloud, it could fry them all. *Geez*, he thought wiping sweat with his sleeve.

In the run-down house, the little girl's cries sounded as though they were right next to him; the filthy paper-thin paneling did little to buffer Waltz from the ugliest sound had ever heard. He had already sold his soul – he told himself as much repeatedly – in order to live on. He would see this part of it through, even if it made him sick.

And after, he would get what he wanted, what he needed. He would take revenge on Cyber who had killed his only friend in the world. He would get answers. He would bring them to justice for bastardizing the remains of Western civilization in order to instill their own selfish power. After.

But before Waltz could get to that point, to that auspicious point, he had to finish his meeting with Nick Reno. Waltz looked at it as his duty; he had agreed to exterminate the deadly cockroach before it spread its rank disease any further.

The radio blasted punk rock riffs that aided and abetted the taped fists that Waltz served up to the lank-haired dope pusher. There were lines of drops sliding down the windows, and to Waltz they seemed to run the color of blood. He paused to listen for a whistle of a missile descending that he could never have heard from where he sat.

* * *

"You're listening to WURL Pirate Radio and don't you forget it!" said the disc jockey.

"Mommy! I WANT MY MOMMYYYY!" cried a child. There was a bright flash that whitened the darkness of the cracked, lopsided room. Thunder followed abruptly.

Ignore it, thought Waltz. *God help me.*

The bricks of cash were passed to the oily hands of the dealer. The smirk shifted and the space below Nick Reno's right eye spasmed. He scratched at the thin line of whiskers above his upper lip and continued to count happily.

How is it possible? He doesn't recognize me. Anxiety tightened Waltz's kneecaps to the point where they really hurt and reminded him of the old running injury that he had never taken care of.

But the new face forgot the knees quickly and curiosity got the better of him. He was the drug dealer. The user. The pusher. The diseased addict. The fixer.

The water pounded on the roof, while doubt pounded his brain. *He doesn't know it's me. Or maybe he does. Maybe he does.*

"Do I know you from somewhere?" Waltz asked. A wet streak of sweat ran down his back.

"Can't say I've had the pleasure, man." But while Reno grasped for the next cash stack he looked Waltz up and down as though he had recognized him. His misty blue eyes narrowed. Reno shifted nervously.

"Maybe in another life" said Waltz breaking the junkie's train of thought and then shivered involuntarily. Reno burped and relaxed his posture.

Waltz had balls. And he knew it. Confidence returned to a respectable level. The women in the crack house depended on him to escape God only knew what torture. But he would get it to work, because he was the dealer and Reno was his partner.

And then a little girl began to sob loudly. She had heard him. His stomach sank and his glance shifted away from the money he was taking out of the duffel bag and toward the warped wooden door in the hall. Reno was watching him closely and saw this.

"You got a problem with my kids?" he asked. Doubt furrowed his brow and his mustache twitched with suspicion.

"None at all" said Waltz. "I'm just a little antsy is all, Mr. Reno."

At that Reno's eyes flickered coldly. He turned and bent down and brought out a Ziploc bag. Waltz noticed how tiny the man's hands appeared this close to his own, as Reno unrolled the plastic carefully and dipped his yellow pinky nail into the powdery red substance. He raised the long fingernail to his nose and inhaled quickly.

"That's the stuff! The good stuff. And do me a favor: call me Nick, please. I'm giving you the best o' the best here, friend. If you're antsy, you're welcome to try some from my own stash – s'on me."

Without a thought, Waltz stepped on the bear trap and felt its bite on his ankle. "No thanks" he said. "Got a long day ahead of me." SNAP. As soon as the words left his mouth, Waltz knew he had made a critical error.

"So you won't get high with me, and you clearly have issue with my young ladies..." said Reno. Sweat poured down Waltz's palms. It was over. The scrawny pusher's right hand disappeared into a backpack at his feet, and Waltz knew that a gun was pointed on him.

Reno did not recognize him, but he still had suspicions of every new client he did business with; it was an observable caution and an integral part of the black market business that could not be overlooked. It was all over.

"I do have a problem with the little girls, Mr. Reno."

To his astonishment, Waltz stopped counting out the stacks of money and sat back and shook his head, as one that is pissed off would do. Reno's body jumped, though the right hand was steady and did not leave its hiding place in the canvas bag.

"In fact, I got a bone to pick with you, Nick" said Waltz in an over-serious tone. Immediately, the tension in Reno ceased. He was still in control and playing part in the other's joke.

"It better be a good bone" laughed Reno.

"How come I hear all of these frightened little girls from behind closed doors?"

"What do you mean?" asked Reno confused.

"I mean you have your own private little peep-house and playroom, Nick, and you do not even invite your old pal Wyatt Holmes to enjoy the show."

"Oh I see!" exclaimed Reno. "You are a bit ballsy, I'll give you that, but you want some fun to help sweeten the pot, so to speak."

"Exactly."

The sweat formed pools in Waltz's hands, and every impulse in his body screamed for him to wipe them on his pants or shirt. But he knew that this junkie was something else besides and far too cunning; he would pick up on the slightest estrangement.

"Well I would apologize, except these are my girls, you understand. Dearly bought. Mine. I don't bring them out to visit with just anybody, and I certainly don't mess around with play during a transaction of this big – uh – quantity when we've only just met this past week."

God, he's offended. This fuck doesn't have a moral to live by, and I've offended him, thought Waltz.

"I don't expect anything of you except your exceptional product, my friend" said Waltz. "Please do not take offense. It's just that I did not expect to be tortured like this during our first meeting."

"Tortured?" asked Reno quizzically.

"I've had a hard-on since that bitch started making noise, Nick." The drug dealer burst out laughing. He slapped his knees jovially and spent thirty seconds catching his breath.

"My dear sir!" he cried. "I admit I liked you from the first. Please allow me to extend this humble offer to you: you see I will not touch a toy once someone else's handled it, but if you would like, I will let you purchase one of my litter at a very low rate since we are now partners on another business front. If you do not want to buy one, you are free to take a long look at each and get high on that, if you will."

"Please!" said Waltz enthusiastically. "I will not be able to concentrate on the counting if I do not free my mind of this temptation."

"Follow me" said Reno.

He turned his back on Waltz and waved a hand to follow him over to the girls' prison. It was the first time Reno had put aside cautions that entire week, and it was his bane.

"Children are the purest innocence on earth you evil fuck" said Waltz, as he grabbed Reno's head and slammed his temple into the doorframe.

UUURRRRRRRRRRRNNNNNN

The sound cannon was deafening. He was sent backward and hit the ground even as Nick Reno was collapsing to the floor beside him. All equilibrium burst in his head.

* * *

Waltz clutched his ears involuntarily. When he could open his eyes and see more than blinding white noise, he noticed that there were two sets of boots on the wooden floor surrounding him. Slowly his eyes regained their focus.

How? he thought.

"Mr. Reno has many hidden cameras throughout the compound. It may look just like an ordinary crack house to you, but that's just subterfuge. Everyone underestimates the boss."

"I know you can hear me now" said Raybo, one of the dealer's hired muscle. "Cameras automatically follow the boss... everywhere. They see everything, at his request. And I love to watch. I don't know why you wanted to hurt him, but when he wakes up you are fucked."

With that there was a savage kick that Waltz did not see coming. The heavy foot landed in his breadbasket and knocked the air right out of him. Silver snowflakes shimmered in his eyes.

He started to turn away and prepare to counter another kick. And then the guards that surrounded him stomped at his torso. They could have easily chosen to break his legs or arms, but there must have been some protocol to maintain whereby Reno got to exact his own revenge on those that threatened him. And Reno probably went about that process slowly and methodically, as it seemed he did everything else. The ruthless bastard might have been a junkie, but he was also an ingenious psychopath.

The kicks subsided. Waltz found it hard to breathe; there must have been broken ribs. The crashing slaps of rain-laden wind hitting the house was loud in the room. One of the men went and attended to Reno. But no one said a word.

And then Waltz heard the injured cry of the little girl pierce his ears again. It was she that had sent him over the edge before. And her audible pain infuriated Waltz more than any vendetta of the government could possibly do. Something, some cord that had held up the baggage of physical anguish for the body in his brain, snapped.

Raybo, the closest goon to Waltz, looked down in surprise as a fast flying foot sent the heel into his balls. Waltz swept the guard's legs out from under him and at the same time dove away from the other guards.

Waltz rose. At first he reeled, but then, with a deep breath, he steadied his feet. Two large, slow goons shuffled forward to crush Waltz. They had the simplest mindset: destroy! But they found that the cyber-warrior was far too quick and agile for them to land a blow, let alone catch him.

Waltz seized an opportunity when a knife hilt stuck out of Raybo's jeans. Thunder crashed. With a spinning and ducking motion, he shot in on Raybo and then over to the other bodyguards and found their throats. Killing strangers was not something Waltz had ever cared for. But he hated Nick Reno more.

The sound cannon bellowed. UUURRRRRNNNNNN. He was pinned against the nearest wall, completely incognizant of direction. The pressure and pain did not subside this time, but instead grew stronger.

A steady maddening ring began to grow in his ears. How could he have forgotten the sound cannon? His vision blurred.

The ring shook his brain. And the god-awful sound got louder. *If it comes any closer my eardrums are going to burst*, he thought.

As permanent deafness grew more and more likely, Waltz was able to look within and cut out the sound and the agony of the torturous weapon. He pictured more than heard the sound of pouring rain thundering down so strongly that rock walls eroded to caves. He focused in on the thump-thump-thump-thump of that rain and found he could think again.

If the ringing and the pressure are increasing, then whoever has the sound cannon is getting closer to me. Based on the damage and disorientation they've gotten close, he thought.

They're in the room now! Why did I forget the sound cannon was there? No, it's too late now, thought Waltz. *Focus, Will... focus... focus... focus. The room's no more than ten by fifteen feet, tops... maybe less. If the cannon's in the room, then they're in range! They're in range!*

And with the blooming of that thought, though he could not see or hear, Waltz reached his belt and activated the hidden EMP blaster in his buckle. As he squeezed the sides of the rectangular metal, there was a vibration, a ZAP, and then blessed relief.

* * *

When he awoke, he found a ringing in his ears that was, luckily, faint, and he hoped that meant that there was not much permanent damage to his hearing. But he was not a doctor.

Waltz sat up slowly in a room of carnage. Two enormous persons were sprawled on the floor and had bled out from their necks; the reddish black liquid still oozed from their wounds. *I could not have been out long then, if they're still bleeding.*

At the opposite end of the room, in a doorway, lay a wiry man with long blond hair straddling his face in clumps, like squid arms. He was on his back and still clutched at the sound cannon in his rigor mortis. The electromagnetic pulse had shorted out the machine he bore and sent fragments of sharp plastic into his jugular where the carotid artery was pierced, and he too had bled out.

Not far from the doorway was another body. It began to move slowly. Nick Reno was alive and starting to crawl.

"Son of a bitch!" cried Waltz.

Standing required an effort and balance required more. But he let the thumping onslaught of rain empower his rage again. Waltz shuffled over to the murderer, the death dealer. He lifted his right leg slowly in the air, as the untouchable Nick Reno lay on the dusty floor trying to get away from him.

Waltz measured, summoned all of his remaining focus and strength, and stepped down with all of his might. The crawling ceased. He dropped his boot, over and over, as the course of two minutes went slowly by. The finality came when there was a CRACK heard that was audible enough that even Waltz could hear it over the ringing in his ears. He had broken Nick Reno's neck.

* * *

When Waltz could walk well enough, he freed the imprisoned women, a mother and her daughter, and walked out the front door not hearing their tearful joy and thanks. The dead bodies could rot for all he cared. They deserved no more than that.

Waltz had fulfilled Xera Finn's vendetta. She had payment. The hard part would be going to her and holding her tight as she allowed the grief of her beloved friend to finally sink in.

89

INEVITABILITY

Outside the nightmare was wet and cold and ongoing. He hoped there was nothing in the water. William Waltz stepped into a deep puddle and was thankful for the Gore-Tex that waterproofed his feet. A subtle paranoia ate away at him.

The strain had mutated. The Ebola did not want to be quelled; it spread. There was no cure, no vaccine.

And so before Waltz secured his helmet, he fixed the bulky gas mask to his face. The straps went around the back of his head and the insectoid-like black skull hid his new face and protected it. Instead of a mouth a thick striated tube snaked down to his belt where a top-of-the-line Oxygen Box eliminated the chance of catching Ebola while riding across the New York islands.

The number of confirmed outbreaks rose every day. Dozens might well become hundreds. And the cyber-attacks became more and more frequent overseas. And the guerilla attacks became more daring and damaging at home.

The rain that fell was hard and strong, as Waltz climbed aboard the long, shining-black bike and shivered. With the press of a button on the dash, below the handlebars, the front-end sank down around him. The angular wings of carbon-fiber-melded armor surrounded his legs and torso. The bike's color shifted to a Ferrari red and seemed to glow brightly on the dark street corner. Waltz hit another button and the color dissolved back to the shiny, but more inconspicuous black.

His gamble that Franciscus' lab could be cleansed – and Cyber's betrayal that started it all – had cost the northwest of what had formerly been the United States of America dearly, as the pandemic raged on. Wangluo was blamed and attacked abruptly. Mayhem ensued.

Cyber, you have betrayed humankind, thought Waltz. *I will not forget. I will not forgive.*

He revved up the Otomo motorcycle and bolts of electricity enveloped the wide tires just before he shot away in lined streaks of color on his way to Manhattan. He was needed. The Cyberwar had begun.

THE END

INDEX

Acknowledgements 8
Prologue 12
1 13
2 15
3 18
4 25
5 30
6 32
7 33
8 35
9 38
10 45
11 48
12 50
13 53
14 56
15 60
16 63
17 64
18 67
19 73
20 75
21 78
22 80
23 84

24..85
25..86
26..88
27..89
28..91
29..94
30..98
31..101
32..103
33..108
34..109
35..111
36..113
37..115
38..119
39..122
40..125
41..126
42..128
43..131
44..133
45..137
46..142
47..143
48..145
49..149
50..153
51..157
52..158
53..162

54 163
55 167
56 172
57 180
58 182
59 187
60 194
61 199
62 202
63 203
64 206
65 208
66 211
67 215
68 218
69 220
70 222
71 223
72 226
73 230
74 233
75 235
76 239
77 241
78 248
79 251
80 253
81 255
82 257
83 259

84 262
85 264
86 266
87 268
88 272
89 282

Made in the USA
Middletown, DE
02 July 2022

68310236R00163